SIMON PULSE
An imprint of Simon & Schuster Children's Publishing Division
1230 Avenue of the Americas, New York, NY 10020
This Simon Pulse edition July 2015
Text copyright © 2015 by Abbi Glines
Cover photograph copyright © 2015 by Michael Frost
All rights reserved, including the right of reproduction in whole or in part in any form.
SIMON PULSE and colophon are registered trademarks of Simon & Schuster, Inc.
For information about special discounts for bulk purchases, please contact Simon & Schuster Special Sales at 1-866-506-1949 or business@simonandschuster.com.
The Simon & Schuster Speakers Bureau can bring authors to your live event. For more information or to book an event contact the Simon & Schuster Speakers Bureau at 1-866-248-3049 or visit our website at www.simonspeakers.com.
Cover designed by Jessica Handelman
Interior designed by Michael Rosamilia
The text of this book was set in Adobe Caslon Pro.
Manufactured in the United States of America
2 4 6 8 10 9 7 5 3 1
This book has been cataloged with the Library of Congress.
ISBN 978-1-4814-2083-9 (hc)
ISBN 978-1-4814-2081-5 (pbk)
ISBN 978-1-4814-2077-8 (eBook)

To my mother, Becky. You've been cheering me on since I was a child with the habit of telling elaborate stories. Thank you for encouraging me to reach for my dreams. I love you.

ACKNOWLEDGMENTS

I need to start by thanking my agent, Jane Dystel, who is beyond brilliant. Signing with her was one of the smartest things I've ever done. Thank you, Jane, for helping me navigate the waters of the publishing world. You are truly a badass.

My editor, Sara Sargent. I've loved working with her on this book. I look forward to working together on many more books to come. Mara Anastas, Jodie Hockensmith, Carolyn Swerdloff, and the rest of the Simon Pulse team, for all their hard work in getting my books out there.

The friends who listen to me and understand me the way no one else in my life can: Colleen Hoover, Jamie McGuire, and Tammara Webber. You three have listened to me and supported me more than anyone I know. Thanks for everything.

I need to give a big shout-out to Abbi's Army, led by Danielle Lagasse. She has pulled together an amazing bunch of readers who promote my books and make me feel incredibly special. I love every one of you, and I am humbled that you would spend your time sharing my books with others.

Natasha Tomic, for always reading my books the moment I type "The End," even when it requires she stay up all night to do it. She always knows which scenes need that extra something to make them a quality "peanut butter sandwich scene."

Autumn Hull, for always listening to me rant and worry, and for still beta reading my books for me. I can't figure out how she puts up with my moodiness. I'm just glad she does.

Last but certainly not least: my family. Without their support I wouldn't be here. My husband, Keith, makes sure I have my coffee and the kids are all taken care of when I need to lock myself away and meet a deadline. My three kids are so understanding, although once I walk out of that writing cave, they expect my full attention, and they get it. My parents, who have supported me all along. Even when I decided to write steamier stuff. My friends, who don't hate me because I can't spend time with them for weeks on end because my writing is taking over. They are my ultimate support group, and I love them dearly.

My readers. I never expected to have so many of you. Thank you for reading my books. For loving them and telling others about them. Without you I wouldn't be here. It's that simple.

Prologue

SIENNA

"Open them wider," Dustin panted in my ear as he pressed my left knee against the leather backseat of his car. I thought we had this down by now, but sometimes he wanted something different. So I had to adjust. Also, keeping my head in the game was hard to do.

In the beginning it had hurt. Now it was just uncomfortable. But I loved Dustin, and he wanted sex. So I gave it to him. Which meant a few nights a week he pinched my nipples really hard, then did the deed and we were done. Being close to him made it worth it. I had felt so disconnected from him lately that this helped ease my mind. When we were back here together, we were okay again.

"Like this?" I asked, moving my leg up to rest along the top of his backseat.

"Fuck, yeah. Like that, baby. Just like that. You're always so damn tight. It's almost impossible to get inside you."

I agreed with him. Which was why it was so uncomfortable. It seemed like there must be something to make it slide in easier. But he never mentioned that, so I didn't ask.

"Fuck, uhhhh, yeah . . . God, babe, so good, uhhhh! GAAAAH!" he cried out loudly as he threw his head back and his eyes rolled into his head.

That meant this was over. He was done. Thank God.

When he moved off me, I quickly sat up in case he wanted to go for round two. I felt like he had made me do splits this time. I didn't want a round two.

"You do know we'll get married one day, right?" Dustin said as he helped straighten my skirt, then handed me my panties.

I had never told him how unsure I was about us having sex all the time, but he knew me too well. He had been my best friend all my life, and when our relationship had progressed into something more, it wasn't a surprise to anyone.

I had loved Dustin Falco since we were kids, so it only made sense that he and I would evolve into this—even if I wasn't sure *this* was what I wanted. Our relationship had changed so much over the past two years.

Or maybe it was just that Dustin had changed so much over the past two years.

Sometimes I didn't recognize him anymore. The boy across

the street wasn't the easygoing, trustworthy friend I'd always adored. He was the record-breaking basketball star who already had college scouts checking him out his sophomore year of high school. Girls wanted him, and boys wanted to be him. He basked in the attention. He knew he was special and he wasn't humble about it.

But I loved him. So I accepted this change. At least, I was doing my best to. Even if it meant he only had time for me when he wanted to have sex. The rest of the time he was busy playing basketball—and drinking with his friends, which was something I wouldn't do. I drew the line at going to the parties he attended. I had gone to two of them with him, and he had gotten so trashed that I had been forced to walk home by myself. If I didn't come home by curfew, my parents would ground me until I turned thirty.

They trusted Dustin, but they had no idea who he really was. Not anymore. My parents would never be okay with me going to parties. My curfew was earlier than everyone else's. It frustrated Dustin, but he always assured me that it was okay, that he'd work around it.

"You're not talking again, babe. That means you're upset. What'd I do this time?" Dustin asked as I tugged my panties back into place.

"Nothing. Just lost in thought. I'm not upset," I assured him. This was what I always did: made sure he was happy and worry free.

He leaned over and touched the side of my face. The gentle look in his eyes reminded me of the boy I'd fallen in love with years ago. "You're my one, Sienna Roy. My one and only. You know that, right?"

I nodded. He had been telling me that since our first kiss. A first kiss that might not have happened if Dustin's older brother, Dewayne, hadn't been showing me attention. It wasn't *that* kind of attention. Not the kind he showed the girls his age. Dewayne was a senior our freshman year of high school. He and his pack of friends ran the school. They owned it.

On our first day of high school, Dustin had left me behind to hang out with the basketball team and the older guys who were more than willing to bring him into the fold. I was the girl who didn't know many people because of my strict parents. Dewayne, however, found me in the hallway at school that day. He helped me get through it. For my first lunch in the big cafeteria, Dustin had gone to sit with his new friends and not had invited me. I was extremely intimidated by the place, so I found a spot by a tree outside to eat my lunch. Alone. Until Dewayne Falco found me and sat down beside me. It was that way for a while. But the more attention he showed me, the more attention Dustin began to show me. Soon I was Dustin's girl.

"I love you, baby. You're my girl. I hate that we have to rush and I can't take you to a bed and surround you with candlelight.

That's what you deserve. It's what I want for you. But right now we have to sneak around your parents. One day you'll be free. We won't have them watching your every move."

I nodded. He was right. One day I would go to college and my father's overprotective eyes wouldn't be trained on me. He would have to let me make my own choices.

"I love you, too," I told him.

He grinned, then leaned in to kiss me. It was a soft peck. After sex Dustin liked to treat me as if I were a treasure. He never wanted me to doubt that he cherished me. It was these few moments that made the rest of it worth it. Because the truth was, I didn't like sex. It was uncomfortable and painful, and I didn't understand why girls liked it so much. From the look on Dustin's face whenever he got off, I could see that it was fantastic for him. But I never had that feeling. Aside from enjoying seeing him feel pleasure, I dreaded having to do it.

"We have fifteen minutes to get you home," Dustin said. This was a nightly ritual with us. He would take me home, then run off to a party or to go play basketball. It was painful to imagine him being around other girls, drinking and staying out late. I had told him once that it worried me that he would get tired of my parents' rules and break up with me. He'd assured me he loved me and only me. Always.

"Fuck!"

I jerked my head around, startled by his outburst, to see him holding up his used condom. The come that was supposed to be neatly inside was coating the outside of the latex.

"Motherfucking condom broke," he swore, before slinging it out the window. "That's the second time this has happened with the box I bought last week. I'm getting a different brand," he grumbled.

"I didn't know another one had broken," I said, trying to remember the time spent in the back of Dustin's car the past week.

His face paled a moment, and then he shrugged. "I didn't want to worry you. It pissed me off and I forgot. But that's twice now. I'll get us new ones. Don't worry," he said with a wink, then tugged his jeans up and fastened them.

"Let's get you home." He opened the door and climbed out, before reaching in and taking my hand to help me. Once we were both standing outside, he wrapped his arms around me and inhaled deeply. "I don't know what I'd do without you, Sienna. I love you so goddamn much. You're my center. You keep me focused and grounded. I can trust you with anything."

This was the Dustin I knew. My best friend. The guy across the street I had known all my life. Not the popular jock who drank too much at parties.

I stood on my tiptoes to kiss him, and he still had to lean down so I could reach his lips. Dustin was already two inches taller than his older brother. The Falco boys were tall. But Dewayne had wider shoulders and the kind of muscles that only men had. Dustin was still a boy. But he was my boy.

Still, that didn't keep me from looking at Dewayne whenever I could get away with it. When Dewayne was outside washing his car, I was up in my room watching from behind the safety of my curtains. Any chance I had of getting a glimpse of Dewayne, I secretly took it.

The day Dewayne sat down beside me at lunch, he had become my hero. He had come to rescue me. And since then he had stepped in and saved me more than once. Having this guy who seemed larger than life always there to help me did things to my heart I couldn't control. Even though I tried to stop feeling things for him. I just couldn't.

I was in love with Dustin Falco, but I was in complete idol worship over his older brother, a fact I could only admit to myself. He was the kind of beautiful that a girl couldn't ignore.

That night after I was tucked into bed and my thoughts drifted to fantasies of Dewayne (because this was the only time I allowed myself to mentally cheat on my boyfriend with his older brother), I heard the sirens. You didn't hear sirens a lot in Sea Breeze. It was a small town, and rarely did the ambulances, police cars, and fire trucks have cause to run off to the same location. But the louder they got, the more serious I realized it

Chapter One

Six years later . . .

SIENNA

I never expected to step foot in Sea Breeze, Alabama, again. When my parents had packed my bags and shipped me off to live in Fort Worth, Texas, with my mom's sister, who I hardly knew, I had been told I would return to Sea Breeze after the baby was born. What I hadn't been told was that they weren't planning on my baby returning with me.

I glanced back at Micah, asleep in his car seat with his Darth Vader action figure clenched tightly in his hand. Our life hadn't been easy, but we had each other. I wouldn't go back and do it any other way. Micah was my life. He had healed me when I was sure nothing ever could.

Keeping Micah meant being disowned by my strict religious parents. My aunt wasn't the most affectionate person in the world, but she'd disagreed with my parents' decision. I had been expected to work and pay my own way, but at least she'd given us a roof over our heads.

Giving up on high school and getting my GED was my only option. My aunt Cathy was the principal at the local high school and helped me get a trade school grant, so when Micah was eighteen months old, I enrolled in beauty school. Before his third birthday I had a degree in cosmetology.

I owed my aunt more than I could ever repay her.

Micah and I moved out just last year and finally got an apartment of our own. I didn't date because I didn't trust anyone around my son. I also felt guilty paying for a sitter when we needed that money for more important things, like rent, day care, and food. It didn't keep men from flirting, though, and trying to get me to go out with them. Janell, the owner of the salon where I worked, said that the men all thought I was playing hard to get. It just made them more persistent.

The truth was, I was lonely sometimes, but then Micah would smile and I'd see his father in him and I'd remember that for ten years of my life I'd had someone. A very special someone. And now I had Micah. I didn't need anything more.

When the call had come two months ago from my mother to tell me about my father's heart attack, I hadn't known what to feel. He had never met Micah, and now he never would. My mother had used Dad's life insurance money to move to a retirement community in central Florida. She'd given her house to Micah and me.

Not one time did she apologize for deserting me when I'd needed her most, or for turning her back on her only grandchild. But the fact that she had given the house to us meant something. I only hoped one day she would realize what she was missing by not knowing him.

Janell had helped me by giving me a glowing reference, and I had managed to get a job in Sea Breeze working at one of the most elite salons in town. I would be making more money, and I wouldn't be paying rent any longer. Our life would be better in Sea Breeze. Micah would get to grow up in the small coastal town that I loved.

My only fear, and the one reason I almost didn't come back home, was the idea of the Falcos seeing Micah. Once I'd realized that my parents hadn't been planning on me keeping my son, I sent a letter to Tabby Falco, Dustin's mother.

She never replied.

The first year of Micah's life I wrote them countless letters and included pictures of him. He looked so much like his father. I wanted them to see that Dustin wasn't completely lost to us. He had left a part of himself behind.

Not once did she respond.

A few times I'd almost worked up the nerve to call them, but if they weren't replying to my letters, then they didn't want to talk to me. They didn't want Micah. It had hurt even worse than my parents not wanting him. I had hated the Falcos for their desertion. But then I learned to let go. Move on. Be happy with my life. With my beautiful little boy.

"Momma? Where are we?" a sleepy little voice asked from the backseat of my twelve-year-old Honda Civic.

"We're home. Our new home," I replied, pulling into the driveway of the house that had once been my home and would soon be again.

"Our new house?" he asked with excitement in his voice as he wiggled in his seat to see better.

"Yep, baby. Our new house. Ready to go inside and see it?" I asked him, opening my car door and getting out. It was a two-door, so I had to lean my seat forward to reach him in the backseat. He unbuckled himself, then scrambled out of his seat and jumped out of the car.

"Do other people live in there too?" he asked, staring up at the two-bedroom wood-frame house with wide eyes.

"Just us, kiddo. You'll have your own bedroom here. Mine is right across the hall from yours."

"Whoa," he said, his eyes shining with amazement. Even when we had lived with my aunt Cathy, Micah and I had shared a room. Once we'd moved into an apartment, a studio was all I could afford with day care costs. This house was only twelve hundred square feet, but it was the biggest living space he and I had ever had all to ourselves. The studio apartment had been a third of this size. We had even shared a bed up until now.

"Let's go see your new room. We might need to paint it. Not sure what color the walls are," I told him. The last time I'd been in my old bedroom, it had been pink. Micah was determined that pink was for girls and wanted nothing to do with it.

From my purse I pulled out the key that my mother had mailed me along with the letter and the deed to the house. I took a deep breath before unlocking the door. Stepping back, I motioned for Micah to go inside. "Check it out."

His grin spread across his face as he took off running into the house, whooping as he saw the size of the living room. Then he turned and headed down the short hallway. I paused at the door, unable to ignore the house across the street any longer, and turned around to look at it. I didn't recognize the truck in the driveway, but then again, it had been six years. I was sure the Falcos were still there. Mother hadn't mentioned that they'd moved.

I wondered if they would speak to Micah when he played in the yard. Or would they ignore him like they had since his birth? I wouldn't tell him who they were. I hadn't told him about my parents. He didn't know this had once been my home. He didn't know he had grandparents. In preschool he had been asked to tell the class about his grandparents, and when he'd told them about Aunt Cathy, he had called her Aunt Cathy. The kids in his class had teased him, telling him that his aunt wasn't his grandparent. He'd come home confused and upset that he didn't know who his grandparents were.

I had just told him he didn't have any.

When he'd asked about his father, I had explained that God had wanted his father because he was such an awesome man, so he had brought him to heaven to live there with him before Micah was born.

That had been enough for Micah. He hadn't asked any more questions. He was happy with the knowledge that his mother loved him unconditionally and that we were a family. It had been hard for him when he saw that other kids had large families, but once he'd understood that each family was different, he was okay with that.

"Momma! Momma!" Micah called out in excitement. "There's a blue room. It's a really cool blue room too! It's even got toys in it already!"

Toys? I closed the front door behind me and headed down the hall. Stepping into the bedroom that had once been mine, I stopped and looked around me in awe. It was blue. A bright, happy blue. It had a full-size bed and a matching wooden dresser. There was a blue quilt on the bed with orange basketballs all over it, and in the center sat a basketball-shaped pillow. A toy box under the window was open, with pirate swords, a baseball bat and glove, a large red fire truck, and what looked like a big bag of Legos sticking out of it. An indoor basketball hoop sat in the opposite corner, with a ball lying on the floor beside it.

Above his bed was painted MICAH.

"Do you think the people who used to live here left it for me? Or do we gotta give it back?" he asked, a hopeful expression on his face. "And look, Momma, my name is already on the wall."

Tears stung my eyes, and I had to swallow hard as I stood there taking in the room. I didn't know what to think. This was not what I had expected, but then again, I hadn't expected to be given this house, either. A white envelope caught my attention. It was leaning against the wall on top of the dresser, with my name and Micah's name written on it.

Walking over to it, I wiped at the tear that had escaped, and I tried to hide my face from my very observant five-year-old. The envelope was sealed, so I slid my finger underneath and opened it up.

Sienna,

This is your home now. It doesn't make up for the past or for the years I wasn't there when you needed me. But it is all I have to give you. I don't expect to buy your forgiveness. This room is as much for me as it is for Micah. I've always wanted to buy him things. Christmas presents and birthday presents and gifts just because he is my grandson. I couldn't do that, though. Not while I lived with your father.

I won't speak ill of your father—that is not what this is about. I loved him. He was a good man, but he was a proud man and I had to respect that. I believe in my heart that if he had it to do over, he would have done things differently. I hate that he never got to meet our grandson.

Please tell Micah that the room is his with love from someone who hopes she can meet him one day. When you are ready, of course. If you are ever ready. I just ask that you can find it in your heart to forgive me. I want to be a part of your lives.

My address and phone number are listed below. If you want to send me a letter or give me a call, I would love that. Or maybe send me some photos of Micah. I have a photo album full thanks to your aunt Cathy. He's a beautiful one, but then, so is his mother.

Love always,
Mom

"Momma, why're you crying?" Micah asked as he tugged on the bottom of my shorts.

I folded the letter and tucked it in my back pocket before bending down and looking at him.

He reached out and wiped my face with his little hands. "It's okay if we can't stay here. Just so I'm with you," he said. The sadness in his eyes hurt my heart.

This house was too good for him to believe. I grabbed his hands and squeezed them tightly. "This is our home. The person who gave it to us did all this just for you. These are happy tears, not sad ones," I told him. I wasn't ready to explain about his grandmother. I didn't know how I felt about introducing him to her. There was too much pain for me to deal with right then. But her words and this room meant a lot. It didn't make up for her abandonment, but knowing she loved Micah enough to do this did help me consider letting her into our life.

"So I get to keep this? All of it?" he asked, looking around at the room again, his eyes wide with wonder.

"Yes. All of this is yours. Just yours. You have your own space now. Your own bed. Even your own closet."

Micah walked over to his bed and ran his little hand over the quilt. He knew what a basketball was. I had bought him one with my first paycheck. It was a part of his father I wanted him to have. "Did the person who did this for me know my daddy was the best basketball player in the world?" he asked, glancing back at me.

I nodded, biting back a smile.

"We're gonna be happy here, Momma," he said, then turned to go back to his toy box. I watched him for a few minutes. I watched him as he dug through the things my mother had left him. Then I slipped out of the room to check out the rest of the house.

In the letter she'd sent with the house key and the deed, she'd told me she was leaving the furniture behind. The place where she was living now was furnished. I wasn't sure how I felt about sleeping on my parents' bed, but all I'd had was a mattress, and we'd left that behind in Texas.

Opening the door to the master bedroom, I froze before relief washed over me. It was my old bed, dresser, and vanity. Even my old desk. She had moved it all into here, knowing I wouldn't want their things. The quilt on the bed was the same one that had been on my bed when I'd left six years ago. It was pale pink with big daisies all over it.

I was home.

Present day . . .

DEWAYNE

I pulled my truck into my parents' driveway and parked beside my dad's truck. Normally, I tried to come over and visit once a week. The past two weeks, however, I just hadn't been in the mood. Momma had broken down and cried the last time I was here, reminding us all that it was the six-year anniversary of my little brother's death.

The only way I knew how to deal with that was to get my ass drunk every damn night until I was numb again. Until I was past the pain, and the empty space in my chest didn't ache so damn bad. After managing to stay sober for the past two nights, I decided I had better get back over here to see my momma before she came looking for me.

That woman had a temper on her, and I didn't need her coming after me. I wasn't scared of much, but Tabby Falco was someone I feared. Loved all five feet three inches of her, but she terrified me.

Glancing across the street, I noticed a beat-up white Honda Civic. It had seen better days. Nina Roy had moved out about a month ago, just a few weeks after her husband's death. Momma said she'd gone to Florida. The place had sat empty for the past month. Was someone moving in? If so, that car didn't make it look like it was the good kind of neighbor. I might have to stop by and make sure my parents were safe.

They didn't need to be dealing with wild parties or a meth house run by some trashy new neighbors. I took a step closer and checked out the license plate. Texas. Now I was as curious as I was concerned. Who the hell did Nina Roy sell her house to? I never even saw a For Sale sign in the yard. If she'd rented it, we might really have a problem. Just last week three rented houses an hour north of here were busted for meth.

"What you gawking at our new neighbor's car for? Get in here and see your momma!" I turned to see my dad standing at the door with it wide open, an annoyed look on his face. Once upon a time I wouldn't have felt the need to protect the man. I wouldn't have thought anything could touch him. But then he'd had the stroke. Things had changed. I had officially taken over my dad's construction company, Falco Construction. Dad just couldn't handle it anymore. He had always seemed larger than life, but nothing had been the same since Dustin's death.

"You met them?" I asked him, nodding toward the house across the street.

He shook his head. "Car showed up. Haven't seen who was in it. No moving van or U-Haul. Just the car. Sometime around noon yesterday. Car was gone at two today when I glanced outside, but then it was back when I went to water the flowers at four."

This was just getting worse. Someone had moved in without stuff. This wasn't the best subdivision in Sea Breeze, but so far it had been safe from things like meth houses. I wasn't about to let that shit find its way into my parents' neighborhood.

"I'll be right back," I told him, and started across the street before he could stop me. Not that he could stop me.

"Get back over here, boy," he called, but I held a hand up.

"Just a sec. I need to check this out," I replied, and kept my eyes focused on the door and the windows. I didn't want to spook whoever was inside and end up getting shot if they were in there setting up shop.

Nina Roy should've thought about who she was letting move into this place. But then, I wasn't sure that woman had much of a heart, anyway. Her daughter had been shipped off shortly after my brother's death, never to return. They'd been best friends for most of their lives, and it had progressed to the relationship stage. Word was, sweet little Sienna had suffered a mental breakdown and they had sent her off to a facility. No one had ever seen her again. It wasn't easy for me to accept for a long time. Much as I hated to admit it, I'd taken her leaving harder than I should have. Especially knowing what Dustin's death had done to her. That was one more thing to add to my list of fuckups.

I knocked on the door and waited. I kept my eyes on the doorknob in case it slowly turned. If the fucker had a gun, I was ready to disarm him. Before I could think about just how I would do that, the door swung open and a pair of brown eyes were looking up at me with keen interest.

"Hi," the little boy said, staring at me as if he wasn't sure he had done the right thing by opening the door.

This was not what I had been expecting. I hadn't imagined a family had moved in across the street, not from the looks of that vehicle. It didn't look like a family car—it wasn't safe for adults, much less kids.

"Hi, your folks home?" I asked him, and he stared at me a moment longer before frowning.

"I don't have folks. I have a momma, but she's in the bathroom. She had to go pee. I probably shouldn't have answered the door."

The kid was cute. And he was right. He didn't need to be

opening the door. Or giving a complete stranger that kind of information. If he had just a mother, then the car in the driveway concerned me for other reasons. If that was all she had, how the hell had she afforded this house? It wasn't an expensive house or anything, but I'd think a used rental trailer would have been more in her price range.

"Maybe in the future you should wait for her to open the door. You got lucky this time." I pointed at my parents' house. My dad was standing on the front porch watching us. "That's my parents' house. I was coming to meet the new neighbors."

The kid peeked around my legs and looked at the house and my dad, then turned his attention back to me. "You live with your parents? My momma ain't got no parents."

Again, more info than he needed to be sharing. Hell, did this woman not teach her kid not to talk to strangers and spill her life story? It wasn't safe.

"Probably shouldn't tell strangers that, either, little man," I told him.

He frowned and held out his hand as if to shake mine. "My name is Micah. What's yours?"

Although he shouldn't have been telling me his name, I couldn't help but grin. The kid was a charmer. I clasped his hand in mine and gave it a shake. "Nice to meet you, Micah. My name's Dewayne."

His grin got huge. "Like Dwyane Wade? You know, from the Miami Heat?"

I didn't keep up with basketball much, but I knew who Dwyane Wade was. I nodded.

"I wish I had a name that cool. But I would want to be named Chris Bosh."

"I take it you're a Heat fan," I said. "Do you play?"

He nodded vigorously. "Oh yeah. I'll be the best one day. My dad was the world's best basketball player. I will be too."

I thought he'd said he didn't have a dad. Just a mom.

"Micah?" a soft, feminine voice called.

The kid's eyes got big and he spun around. "Yeah, Momma. I'm at the door with our neighbor. He came to visit."

I lifted my eyes from the kid just in time to see legs. Long fucking legs, all smooth and creamy and encased in tiny little cutoff blue jean shorts. Holy hell. My eyes continued their upward track, taking in the tiny waist and generous breasts barely covered up by a tank top before reaching her face.

Mary, Mother of Jesus. No. Fucking. Way.

I knew that face. It was older. She was a woman now, but I knew that face. Those bright blue eyes, all that long, silky red hair, and those pink lips that made men, young and old, fantasize. But this . . . She couldn't— I stopped and stepped back, and then my eyes returned to the boy in front of me.

"Micah, go to your room," she said in a calm, even voice. "Now. Go."

"But he's nice—" the little boy started, but she cut him off.

25

"Micah, go."

I watched the back of his head as he walked away from me. I wanted to see his face again. I wanted to study it. This was not . . . This couldn't . . . No. He was too young. He wasn't Dustin's. There was no way she'd had my brother's kid and hid him from me . . . from us. But the kid had said his dad was a basketball player. He'd never known Dustin. He obviously knew his dad.

"Hello, Dewayne," Sienna said, with a tone of warning I didn't miss. My head was still reeling. How did she have a kid? I thought she'd lost her mind when my brother had died. Not gone off and started a family.

I stared at her. I didn't understand. I was trying to wrap my brain around it. How old was that kid? Where the hell was his father? Men didn't let women like this one walk away. Especially with a kid that damn cute.

"Sienna," I finally said. "It's been a long time."

Chapter Two

DEWAYNE

"Freshman girls," Preston Drake drawled, sounding pleased as he looked down the hallway. "Damn shame they'll be illegal before the year is over. We need to enjoy being seventeen while we can."

Marcus elbowed Preston in the ribs. "Dude, you're a douche. Glad my sister won't be here until next year when we're gone."

Preston chuckled. We all knew he wasn't going to touch Amanda Hardy. She was our little sister too. Or at least, it felt like it. We'd been friends with Marcus since Amanda was in diapers.

"Y'all seen Trisha?" Rock asked as he walked up to us with a frown firmly in place. It was the kind of frown that meant he was on the verge of beating the shit out of someone.

"No. She didn't take the bus?" Marcus asked.

Rock shook his head. "Stupid piece-of-shit mother of hers. I'm gonna have to go find her. I'll be back later. Cover for me," he said, before turning and heading for the back exit of the building. This was a once-a-week thing. Trisha had a verbally abusive mother, and her mother's current boyfriend had slapped Trisha's younger brother, Krit, around last week. Trisha had jumped on the man's back and started pulling his hair, and he'd slung her across the room. If Rock hadn't shown up when he did, Trisha would have ended up in the hospital or worse. Rock was working on getting her out of there. But he had to do something about her younger brother, too. She wouldn't leave him in a dangerous situation.

"Ain't that Dustin's girlfriend?" Marcus asked, drawing my attention back to the present moment. I scanned the people until I saw Sienna Roy standing in the crowd with her book bag held protectively to her chest and her eyes wide with wonder. She looked lost. Where the fuck was my brother? The girl had turned into a beauty overnight. I had told him just last month he needed to make their relationship official before they started high school. Guys were going to notice her.

"Yeah, it is, and the stupid little fucker isn't anywhere around," I muttered. Sienna was so damn overprotected by her parents that she didn't have much of a life outside of her house and ours. My brother was already going to parties, but Sienna didn't get to go. And she never seemed to have friends over. Dustin was her friend. But his stupid ass was nowhere to be found.

"They break up?" Preston asked, taking a new, keen interest

in Sienna. Fuck no. He could back his horny ass off.

"They were never a couple. And don't even go there. I'll beat your ass. Do you understand me?"

Preston gave me that cocky grin that I'd hate if he wasn't one of my best friends. Right now, though, I was considering knocking it off his face.

"Don't piss him off, Preston. I'm not in the mood to handle that without some backup," Marcus said, glaring at Preston.

I wasn't going to let my little brother leave Sienna out there to the dogs. And there were lots of fucking dogs at this school.

"I'll meet y'all in first period. I got something to do," I told them but didn't make eye contact. I didn't want to see the looks on their faces. I never messed with freshmen. But this one freshman needed me, and if my brother wasn't going to take care of her, I was.

I didn't have to shove through the crowd. It split for me as I made my way to Sienna. I was halfway there when her gaze found me. First her eyes went wide with surprise, and then a shy smile touched her face. Damn, she was pretty. Too damn pretty. My brother was an idiot.

"Hey, Little Red, looks like you found your way to the big leagues," I teased her as I took her arm gently and pulled her to the side of the busy hallway. "You found your locker yet?"

She blushed and glanced down at her feet. I followed her gaze and noticed she was wearing a pair of cowboy boots with her skirt. That was sexy as hell. Fuck! She was a kid. She was also my brother's girl. He just needed to grow up and realize it.

"I looked for it, but there are so many people, and I couldn't remember if the one hundreds are on the first or second floor. So I just figured I'd carry my books around today and stay late to find it."

Her books weighed more than she did. "What's your number?" I asked her. I wasn't letting her carry those books around all day.

"One eighty-eight," she said, frowning and looking around again. The hall was so full of people, it would be hard to see the locker numbers from her height.

"Come on. Can't have you getting a backache your first day of school," I told her, and put my hand on her back to guide her through the crowd. I could see people looking at us, and I wanted to glare at them all and warn them to be careful with her. But I didn't. I made my threat silently. I kept my hand on her back as we walked down the hall and turned left to find her locker in the first row on the east wing.

"This is it. You got the combination?"

She looked relieved. She dropped her bag and began going through it until she pulled out a little scrap of paper. "Here it is," she said, beaming at me before carefully turning the lock until it popped open. I took the door from her and made a little change to the inside of it.

"Now close it. Let me show you something," I told her.

She closed it without question and looked up at me.

"Hit it twice."

She barely slapped at it.

Chuckling, I shook my head. "No, Little Red. You got to hit it twice. Like this." I showed her, then turned the lock once and it opened up.

Her eyes went wide. "How'd you do that?"

Winking at her, I grabbed her book bag and put it inside the locker. "Magic, sweetheart." I closed the door again. "Now you try it again."

She hit it harder this time, and with one twist of the lock it popped open. She laughed and clapped her hands in excitement. "That is so cool. Thank you, Dewayne."

Yeah, my brother was going to have to do something fast, because this kind of pretty wasn't going to be left alone long. I'd have to make sure no one else got near her until Dustin woke the fuck up.

Present day . . .

SIENNA

I had wanted to prepare myself for this. I needed time to think this through. Had the Falcos sent Dewayne over here to look at Micah? To see if he was Dustin's? Was that what this was?

My stomach turned, and I was sure I was going to throw

up right there at his feet. Micah didn't know them. They hadn't made any attempt to know him. I couldn't just let them try to walk into his life. Not like this.

"It has been a long time. Why are you here?" I replied, not taking my eyes off Dewayne. He was still larger than life. More so than when I was a teenager. He had a few more piercings now and a couple more tattoos. His shoulders were even wider, and the thick, corded muscles in his arms were intimidating. The man was like a brick wall.

Yet those eyelashes of his were still too long for a male, and even though he'd pierced his lip, it didn't take away from the plumpness that women paid good money to mimic. The worn jeans that looked like they needed a good washing hugged him in a way I wanted to ignore. I had to ignore. This man was off-limits to me.

He wasn't just the nice guy who had been my friend when I was younger. He was also a man who had abandoned me when I'd needed someone the most. Even if he was delicious and what female fantasies were made of, I would never forgive him. Dustin had adored him, yet Dustin's son didn't even know him.

He cocked an eyebrow at me, as if he was surprised by my reaction to him. "Came over to see who the new neighbors were. Beat-to-shit car parked out front concerned me. Neighborhood's not what it used to be."

Once I wouldn't have been able to look past his perfectly

chiseled face and full lips to get angry with him. That wasn't the case any longer. My hands fisted at my sides, and I wanted nothing more than to punch him in the nose. I owned that car. I had worked hard to buy that car.

"I'll keep that in mind. I can assure you we're not going to cause any problems," I replied, putting my hand on the door to let him know I was done with this visit and wanted him to leave.

Dewayne frowned, and his dark eyes, which in my dreams had looked at me like he had today when I'd walked into the room, were now narrowed. Great, I'd managed to piss off a massive, monster-size man who could knock me down with one hard puff. "Where did that sweet girl I used to know go? You lose her somewhere?" Dewayne's voice was even, but the low, menacing sound of it bothered me.

What did he expect me to do? Bat my eyelashes at him and swoon like I had when I was a kid? "She learned to toughen up and trust no one." I gripped the door, fighting the urge to slam it in his face. Because I was pretty sure he could rip it off its hinges if provoked. "Thanks for stopping by. Now that you know we aren't about to dirty up the neighborhood with our presence, you can go on back to your parents' place. We're fine here." I started closing the door. Dewayne stepped back. To my surprise, he turned around, then started walking away.

At least he took the hint. I was torn between being angry and being relieved. He'd left without making a scene and upsetting

Micah . . . but he hadn't asked me one thing about him. Hadn't asked to see him or asked for his parents to get to meet him. That was a pain I thought I'd gotten over years ago. Now I realized I hadn't. Living here was like ripping the scab right off. It hurt something fierce.

Locking the door, I moved over to peek through the curtains and saw Dewayne talking to his dad as he walked inside their house. Why were they like this? I had loved them like my own family. At times growing up, I'd wished they *were* my family. Tabby had always had a smile and open arms when I needed to throw myself into them. Never would I have imagined that the child of the son they'd adored would be completely ignored.

Micah was so special. He had his father's charm, and he was so smart. He was like a little grown man in a child's body. Everyone who had ever met him fell in love with him. Just like his father. His smile was Dustin's, and so was his laugh. It was like having a part of Dustin with me all the time. But Micah was his own person, and he had wonderful qualities his father hadn't had. He was perfect.

Dustin would have wanted Micah to have his last name. That would never be. I did the only thing I could do and gave him his father's given name instead. Micah Dustin Roy was what I put on his birth certificate. Back then I had hoped that one day the Falcos would allow me to change his last name to Falco. That dream had passed years ago.

"Momma?" Micah's voice was filled with concern.

I walked over to him and squatted down to his eye level. He knew he shouldn't have answered the door. It was something I had drilled into his head since we'd moved out of Aunt Cathy's. We still had to talk about this. Just because he felt safe here didn't mean there was no danger.

"You know better than to open that door," I told him.

His shoulders slumped and he nodded. "Yeah. I know. I forgot. But that man was nice. He wasn't a bad guy, was he, Momma?"

I thought about that. Dewayne wasn't a bad guy the way that Micah meant. But he wasn't a good man. A good man wouldn't have turned on his brother's child. "He's not someone we need to spend time with. He won't hurt us or anything, but I don't trust him. Our business is our business. That's it. Okay? We don't share our business with anyone. When someone comes into our life who I feel we can trust, I will let you know. Until then, it's just me and you."

Micah nodded. "Okay. Just me and you."

I held up my fist. "Dynamic Duo," I said.

He fisted up his hand and bumped mine. "Dynamic Duo," he repeated. Then he threw his arms around me and hugged me tightly. "Love you, Momma."

"I love you, too, baby boy."

I held on to him as long as he would let me. When he was

done, he dropped his arms and stood back. "I'm gonna go back to my room and play."

I stood up and pressed a kiss to his head. "I'm gonna fix us some supper," I told him.

"Mac 'n' cheese!" he called out as he ran for his room.

"No. You're gonna turn into mac 'n' cheese," I called back to him, laughing, before heading to the kitchen. Tonight we were eating bread pizzas. It was something I had come up with to make a cheap meal interesting. Slices of sandwich bread with tomato paste, cheese, pepperoni, and mushrooms didn't cost much and made several meals.

"You're gonna make bread pizzas, aren't you?" he said as he stuck his head back out of his room and looked down the hall toward the kitchen.

"Yep. You gonna help me?"

"Yup!" he called back. "You don't put enough cheese," he explained as he came running back toward me.

DEWAYNE

"What's the verdict? You think the kid who answered the door is gonna be the new neighborhood drug lord?" Dad asked as he followed me into the house.

I shot him an annoyed glare and he chuckled. He didn't realize that shit actually went on in some places. It was my job to keep them safe, even if he didn't accept that.

"Looked right terrifying. 'Specially when he peeked around your legs at me."

The kid had been cool. Dad would love him. . . . But . . . I wasn't sure I was gonna tell him just who that kid belonged to. Sienna wasn't the same girl they'd known. She was cold, distant, and hiding something. I knew enough about people to know when someone wanted to get rid of me because they didn't want me to see too closely.

The boy had to be what had made her clam up. She didn't want us to know she'd turned around and gotten knocked up, probably no more than a year after Dustin was killed. Can't say I blame her, because it didn't look real good. Maybe she really had snapped, and because she was mentally unstable, she'd made a mistake and ended up with Micah.

She sure didn't look mentally unstable now. Fuck. Who was I kidding? The woman could be crazy as a loon and I wouldn't have noticed. Her body and that gorgeous face of hers had hindered my seeing the real her. She was the kind of good-looking that made guys not give a shit if she was insane.

But the boy had been normal. Happy, even. Didn't look scared or neglected. A crazy momma couldn't raise such a normal-acting kid. Could she? Was he even hers? Could that be her secret, that she was raising someone else's kid?

"That brain of yours sure is a-workin'. The tiny tike drug lord worrying you?"

I shook my head and rolled my eyes at my dad.

"Is that Dewayne I hear? Did my boy finally come see me?" Momma's voice called out from the kitchen. The guilt swamped me as she came around the corner, smiling like I had just lit up her world, and opened her arms to me. I was the only kid she had now. Not the one who was going to be a star and make them proud. I was the tatted-up rebel who had planned on raising hell and traveling the world with nothing but a backpack. No reason to stay anywhere long.

But then the good son, the one who had been meant for greatness, got drunk and ran his car into a fucking tree going more than a hundred miles an hour. Now she had me. I was it. And I was still a fuckup even though I tried like hell to do the right thing. Make her proud.

"Sorry, Momma. I should've slowed down long enough to get over here. Won't happen again," I told her as I returned her hug. The top of her head didn't even touch my chin.

"Good. I missed you," she said, stepping back and then swatting me with the dish towel in her hand. "I'm about to pull the apple pie out of the oven and run it over to the new neighbors. Then we can sit down and eat."

Fuck. I hadn't thought about Momma and her apple pies. Of course she'd want to take one to Sienna. I needed to prevent that. Bad idea. Momma was still too raw from the anniversary of Dustin's death. She didn't need to see her new neighbors just yet.

"Yeah, not gonna happen tonight. I just went over there and met them. They were headed out to dinner and to get some groceries. Didn't seem much to want company. Really odd woman."

Momma frowned and then shrugged. "Then y'all can eat my pie and I'll make another tomorrow and see if I can't get it over there to them. Shouldn't be calling the poor woman odd, though."

She turned and walked back toward the kitchen, and I followed behind her. I knew there would be beer in the fridge, and I needed one.

"All I saw was legs, but from the look of them, wasn't nothing about them legs odd," Dad said behind me.

The old man loved to cause problems. He found that shit funny. "Legs were okay, I guess, but the rest of her was average. Nothing special," I lied.

I so fucking lied.

Chapter Three

Eight years ago . . .

DEWAYNE

"Dude. Seriously. Fuck." Preston's tone of voice caught my attention, and I looked up from unlacing my football cleats to see what he was so excited about.

Ellie Nova was headed our way. And she was smoking hot. But then, Ellie was always smoking hot. When she'd moved here our freshman year, we'd all walked around with hard-ons, hoping to get a glimpse up those short skirts of hers or a go at her tits. Which were fucking huge.

"I want some of that. Before we graduate, I want that pussy," Preston said in a low voice.

The problem with Ellie was that she had a whole shit ton of money and she was a princess. No, she was a fucking queen. She looked down her nose at everyone. Didn't matter—guys still fantasized about her. She was Sea Breeze High's own centerfold.

"Good luck. I think she may be the only ass in our senior class you haven't tapped—and the only one you never will," I said. I loved rubbing it in to pretty boy that Ellie hadn't given him the time of day.

"Okay, first of all, I've not tapped ugly ass. I have standards. And second of all, I'll get between those thighs before we leave this place. I'm Preston Drake," he reminded me, with a cocky shrug and a smirk.

Truthfully, if any of us was going to lay Ellie, it would be Preston. I had no doubt.

"Dewayne," Ellie's voice said, startling me, and I turned to look at her. I was pretty sure she'd never actually said my name in four years.

"Yeah?" I replied, refusing to let her know I wanted a taste.

She twirled a lock of golden hair around her finger and nibbled on her bottom lip as she looked up at me through long lashes. I didn't even care if those lashes were fake. This was a hot look. A very fucking hot look.

"I was wondering if maybe you could give me a ride home," she said with a pouty mouth.

I could give her a ride, all right. One she wouldn't soon forget.

"Fuck that," Preston cursed behind me. This was going to drive him nuts.

I couldn't help but grin. "Sure. Just let me get my bag out of the locker room," I said, trying not to act like I was happy about this. Playing it cool with Ellie was the only way I'd get what I wanted out of her.

"Thank you so much. My car's in the shop, and I didn't want to call Daddy to come get me."

I didn't want her calling Daddy either. I had plans that I was sure Daddy wouldn't approve of.

Preston shoved me as I walked by him, and I bit back a laugh. This was so pissing him off. And I'd have it to rub in his face for the rest of our lives. I got between Ellie's legs first. Because that was the game plan. I wanted to see if that stuck-up, hot-as-fuck pussy was worth all the attention it got her.

"Hey, Sienna, what's up with you, girl? Come looking for me?"

Preston's words stopped me, and I turned back around to see Sienna looking unsure as she smiled that sweet, shy smile at Preston. Then she looked at me. Damn. That smile. It made something in me clench up like a motherfucker every time. Did she realize that?

"I, uh, was going to see if I could get a ride. I missed the bus and Dustin has already left, I think. I didn't see him much today, and I don't know where he goes after school," she said, her cheeks turning pink as she looked at me.

"Yes, beautiful, you sure as hell can. I was just thinking I hated riding home alone," Preston replied in that sugary-sweet tone that was meant to goad me. He was getting his revenge. Or he thought he was.

"No," I said, walking over to Sienna to take her arm. "I'll get Sienna home. You take Ellie home," I told him, making sure he understood I wasn't fucking around.

Preston understood. His smirk was more than pleased. He'd be fucking Ellie first after all. And after this I was pretty damn sure I'd never get a taste of Ellie Nova. But she wasn't important enough to ignore Sienna for. If Sienna needed me, I couldn't find it in me to tell her no. And I sure as fuck wasn't letting Preston around her. Alone. Hell no.

Present day . . .

SIENNA

By Friday we had found our rhythm. Micah got up and dressed himself while I made breakfast, which consisted of a Pop-Tart and a glass of milk. That wasn't going to win me Mom of the Year, but he liked Cookies & Creme Pop-Tarts, and I liked getting him to school on time. We did eat breakfast together. I ate my breakfast bar and drank some coffee while Micah chatted away happily.

I was not a morning person. I couldn't even form words until I'd had at least thirty minutes of wake-up time and two cups of coffee. Micah, on the other hand, woke up singing. This morning he had told me his predictions for the upcoming basketball season. I'd had no idea what he was saying, but I nodded and sipped my caffeine.

Getting myself dressed took more time, but it gave Micah a chance to play with his toys and pick out what he wanted me to pack him for lunch. He liked having choices. Most days we didn't have many choices, but he still wanted to pick them out.

He hadn't been late once all week, and neither had I. My new job was Tuesday through Saturday. Micah went to after-school care until five every day. The counselor at his school had told me about it. The cost was determined by my income, so it was much more affordable than a day care.

An added bonus was that several of the kids from his class went to after-school care too. So he enjoyed getting to play with his new friends. If it weren't for the fact that I had to see the Falcos' house every day, this would all be perfect. But seeing Dustin's house continually reminded me of the rejection that Micah didn't deserve from people whose blood he shared.

"Sienna . . . Roy?" a familiar voice said, breaking me out of my thoughts while I was sweeping up the hair from my last appointment. Lifting my head, I reminded myself that I was prepared for this. People were going to recognize me. Just because I had gone a week without being recognized (aside from Dewayne) didn't mean it wasn't going to happen eventually.

Amanda Hardy smiled at me as she tucked her long, shiny blond hair behind her ear. Her eyes sparkled with actual pleasure to see me. But then, that was Amanda. She'd been a year behind me in school, but her older brother, Marcus, was a close friend of Dewayne's and I had gotten to know her through him. She had always been pretty, but she was gorgeous now. I hadn't seen her since she was fifteen. The diamond on her left hand caught the sunlight. Not surprising that she was engaged. I imagine the guys around here had beaten down her door—that is, if they'd been able to get past Marcus.

I leaned the broom against my work station and walked over to where she stood at the receptionist desk. "Hello, Amanda," I said.

She pulled her designer purse up on her arm and kept beaming at me like I was the lost ark and she'd found me. In my head I ran through the wealthy guys around here who could have afforded to put a ring on her finger. She was sweet, but she was also a diva. Always had been.

"I didn't know you were back in town. And you're working here? I can't believe it. You were just gone. . . ." She stopped, and the sadness in her eyes reminded me that she had been close enough to the Falcos through Marcus that she remembered how painful that had been.

"My mother retired and moved to Florida. She gave me the house. I thought it was time I came home," I explained. I had no idea what my parents had told people. I knew they hadn't told them the truth. At least, I assumed they hadn't. I feared they may have told other people what I'd heard my mother tell Dewayne. I hoped not.

Her frown deepened, and the pity in her eyes put out the earlier twinkle. "I heard about your dad. I'm sorry."

I nodded. I wasn't sure what else to say. My anger at him was still there. He'd taken my son's family away from him. The love Micah deserved had been stolen from him because of my father.

"Manda, how long did you say you'd . . ." *Preston.* The trademark blond hair that belonged to none other than Preston Drake was the first thing I noticed.

His eyes went from Amanda to me, and then they went wide in surprise. Preston was also one of Dewayne's close friends. That group of four guys had owned Sea Breeze High their senior year. Most girls drooled over Preston—he'd been the heartbreaker. But not me. My fascination had been with Dewayne. Preston had done nothing for me.

"Holy shit! Is that you, Sienna?" Preston asked as he stepped inside and walked toward us.

Apparently, Dewayne hadn't told anyone he'd seen me. I would not accept the fact that it hurt. He had proved already how much he didn't care. I didn't know why I was surprised.

"Yes, it's me," I replied just as Preston's arm wrapped around Amanda's waist and he tugged her against him, then kissed her temple. No way. No freaking way. Marcus would kill him. Wouldn't he? Preston had slept with most of Sea Breeze, and

Marcus knew that better than anyone. How was he walking around and kissing on Marcus's little sister?

Amanda giggled, and Preston's grin grew.

"How are you alive?" I asked him as they both looked amused at the shock on my face.

"Oh, he beat my face in. But then he got over it and accepted it. We didn't give him much choice," Preston said.

I simply nodded, then looked back at Amanda. "So that ring is . . ."

"Preston Drake is getting hitched. Hard to believe, isn't it?" she said in a teasing tone, then pinched Preston's waist.

"Watch it, sexy," he said, gazing down at her like she was the most precious thing on the face of the earth.

Had I ever had a guy look at me like that?

No.

I hadn't. The only love I knew was the love of a boy. He'd never had a chance to become a man. I had no idea what being loved by a man felt like. And until this moment I would have said I didn't care, but watching these two, I wondered if I would ever know that feeling.

"It's good to see you. Glad you're back in town," Preston said, then turned his attention back to Amanda. "Call when you're done. I'll come back and pick you up, yeah?"

She nodded. He kissed her fast and hard, then headed for the door.

The silly grin on Amanda's face as she watched him go just brought home the fact that I didn't know that kind of love and I probably never would. Didn't matter, though. I had Micah. He was so much more.

"Sorry. He's clingy today because I've been gone for two days, wedding gown shopping in Manhattan with Sadie, a friend of mine."

I nodded like I understood, but "shopping" and "Manhattan" were foreign words to me. I bought stuff at the local Walmart.

"Do you have an appointment with someone?" I asked. I didn't want to be rude, but I still hadn't taken my lunch break and it was already three.

"Yes, with Hillary at three fifteen," she replied.

Hillary was the owner. She had trained in New York, Los Angeles, and Paris. The fact that she had even hired me was a miracle. I was good at what I did, I knew that, but I wasn't trained like she was.

"I'm here," Hillary called out as she walked from the back room. Her long red hair was not at all natural, but it was exotic. Add to that her crystal-blue eyes, her eyelash extensions, and the collagen in her lips, and she was a head turner.

Amanda waved at her, then smiled at me. "I'm so glad you're back. We need to get together sometime. Maybe go out one night."

I wouldn't be going out at night. Leaving Micah wasn't an

option. I nodded instead because I didn't feel like telling her about Micah yet. She would ask questions I didn't want to answer yet. Besides, anyone who knew Dustin and took one look at Micah would know.

DEWAYNE

The condos were going to be finished on time. One less worry on my mind. After the tropical storm that came through in July, I was afraid it was going to put us off a month or so. Investors were getting nervous, and all that came to rest on my shoulders. Fucking idiots should have considered the fact that weather slows shit down before promising buyers that the place would be ready before Christmas. Dumbasses.

Pulling off my hard hat, I stepped out onto the parking lot from the building and headed for my truck. I was done for the day. The crew was rolling and didn't need me. I'd been out here since five this morning. Squinting against the sun, I was able to make out Preston leaning up against my truck with a smirk on his face. Why was he here? He never showed up at my work sites.

"Just dropped Manda off to get her hair done," Preston said, looking at me pointedly.

I had no fucking idea what this was about, so I just stood silently and waited for there to be a point to this.

I saw the moment when it finally dawned on him that I had

no clue what he was talking about. He pressed his lips together, then shook his head. "You might want to stop by. Say hello," he said. "Sienna is back."

I should have known. Each day that passed without my mother calling to yell at me for not telling her that the new neighbor was Sienna, I breathed a sigh of relief. But it was only a matter of time before people in town saw her. And what the hell was she doing at Hillary's salon? That place was expensive, and from the look of Sienna's car, she didn't need to be paying high prices for her damn hair. What about the kid?

"She have her kid with her?" I asked, trying to make the disgust in my voice not too obvious.

"Kid? What? Fuck! She's got a kid? She married?"

She didn't have her kid with her. Fan-fuckin'-tastic. She'd left the little boy at home alone. What the hell kind of a mother was she?

"And you knew she was back? With a kid? Why haven't you said anything?"

"She moved into her parents' house. I met her kid when I went over there to check out the neighbors for my parents. Didn't think it was important that she was back. She was a part of Dustin's life, not mine," I replied, then jerked open the truck door.

"Liar. Fucking full-of-shit liar. You watched over that girl for years. Hell, when she was a freshman, you acted like her damn guard dog. When she was sent away, it fucked with your head. You were grieving for Dustin, and then she was gone and you grieved for her, too. I would have thought you'd care that she was back. Unless she's married and that's why you're pissed."

Pretending like I hadn't been super invested in Sienna and her happiness back then was pointless. My friends knew the truth, even if my brother hadn't noticed. "She's not married," I replied, and climbed into the truck. "But the girl I cared about is gone. A cold bitch is in her place. And if she's getting her hair done at Hillary's, then she's a selfish bitch. The piece-of-shit car she drives isn't safe for her boy to ride in."

I started to close the door, but Preston grabbed it. "Whoa, man, what's your deal? She's got you acting like an ass, and you're not an ass. Sienna is working at Hillary's, not getting her hair done."

Maybe I *was* an ass.

"Oh," I replied, wishing I hadn't snapped in front of Preston.

"Yeah, *oh*. Sienna didn't seem like a bitch at all. She seemed nice. . . . She was Sienna."

No, she wasn't. She was a mother, and she was fucking hiding something.

And if she was working, where the hell was Micah?

"I'm tired. I need a beer and then my bed. I'll see you later," I told him.

"Live Bay tomorrow night?" he asked.

Live Bay was the club in town were we all used to drink and pick up women. Now it was just me picking up women. The rest of those assholes were hitched or as good as hitched. "Yeah. I'll see you there," I told him as I closed the door. Then I headed to my parents'.

I could tell myself I was going to visit my momma, but the truth was, I was going to make sure Micah wasn't at home alone. Something about the way Sienna had sent him away from me and gotten defensive bothered me. I wasn't convinced the woman was mentally stable.

Once I got to my parents', I parked beside my dad's truck and made my way across the street before he realized I was here. I didn't want an audience, nor did I want his commentary.

Sienna's car was gone, so she wasn't home yet. *That kid had better not be here.* I walked up the steps and knocked on the door. I waited a full minute, and nothing. So I knocked again. Why I was completely convinced she'd left her kid at home I wasn't sure. I didn't know Sienna. I didn't actually have proof she was crazy.

"Micah, you in there? It's Dewayne. I thought I'd stop by and check on you," I called out, but there was only silence.

He wasn't in there. I was overreacting. Why? I didn't have a fucking clue. I turned and headed back down the stairs just in time for the beat-up Honda to pull into the driveway. Great. Now I had to explain myself.

Her car door opened and she stepped out. The sunglasses perched on her nose covered up those eyes of hers, so I had no idea what she was thinking. She bent down and then stood back up. I could see the small head scrambling out of the backseat and then heard his feet hit the pavement.

"Dewayne!" he called as he ran around the front of the car with an excited grin. But then he stopped. His smile vanished, and he stiffened and glanced back at his mother.

Sienna closed the car door and walked toward Micah. She rested her hand on his shoulder, bent down to whisper in his ear, then handed him the keys.

He nodded. "Okay," he said glumly, then headed toward the house, not looking up at me again. When he got to the door, he unlocked it and went inside.

"What are you doing here?" she asked in her very unwelcoming tone. Apparently, the friendly smile she'd had for Preston was not happening for me.

Now, I could either lie to her or tell her the truth. I wasn't a liar. "Heard you were working. I was concerned the kid was home alone."

The expression on her face went from shocked to downright pissed. "Alone? You . . . you think that I would leave my son alone?" she asked in a horrified voice. "I'm not an idiot. And if you haven't noticed, I'm the only family he has. I'm the only one who wanted him and loved him. So don't"—she pointed her finger at me, her voice rising as fury simmered in her eyes—"act like you give a shit about him now. You *do not* have the right. Get away from here. Go back over to that house. Forget about what your brother would have wanted. Pretend that abandoning me and his son when we needed *someone* was okay." She was breathing so hard her chest was heaving, and tears had filled her eyes. Then she was running past me, and I couldn't stop her. I couldn't fucking move.

Hell . . . I couldn't fucking breathe.

"Momma?" Micah's voice called, and I moved then. I spun around and looked at him. Sienna wiped at her face with her arm and bent down to press a kiss to his head and whisper something to him.

He wrapped his little arms around her, and then he turned his head and glared at me. He actually glared at me. My chest exploded into a million pieces as I stood there and stared into the eyes of my brother's son. How had I not seen it? His eyes were just like Dustin's.

"Don't come back here. You made my momma cry!" he yelled at me.

Sienna leaned back and grabbed his little arms gently and started talking to him again. He nodded and turned to go back inside. She stood up and glanced back at me.

The pain in her eyes confused me. Her words confused me. Why did she think we knew about this? Why was she blaming us for not being a part of his life? We didn't know. She'd left and never come back.

"He's Dustin's," I said as the reality of this finally sank in.

She frowned, and then she slowly nodded.

I dropped my head into my hands and took several deep breaths. Holy fuck, I had to get control of myself. One emotion after another slammed into my chest. Pain, guilt, anger, disbelief—but more than anything, pure joy. It trumped all the other emotions. For six years I had mourned my brother. It had changed the way I lived my life. There had been only the memories and the mind-numbing guilt that I hadn't been paying enough attention to his bad choices. I had picked a fucking fight with him, and he'd run off behind the wheel drunk. If I had just paid attention to him, he could be alive right now. It was a solid weight on my shoulders keeping me from finding any joy in life. But now . . .

I dropped my hands and stared back up at Sienna.

Her little boy was a part of Dustin. My brother wasn't completely gone anymore. He'd left behind something . . . someone.

This didn't bring him back, but for the first time in six years my heart felt lighter. Not just for me, but for my family.

Chapter Four

SIENNA

He hadn't known about Micah.

He didn't have to tell me that. It was all over his face. Only once in my life had I seen this intimidating man look on the verge of crumbling, and that had been at Dustin's funeral. How had he not known? Had his mother not told him?

"Momma? You coming?" Micah asked, sounding worried. I had to get inside with him. This was not the place for this. Micah was my first concern, always.

"I can't do this here," I told Dewayne. "He doesn't need to hear it."

Dewayne's eyes shifted to the door, but Micah was already inside. Dewayne couldn't see him. I watched as he swallowed hard and the hint of his Adam's apple moved. Then he nodded and looked back at me. "Okay, but I have questions. He's . . . he's . . . I want to know him, Sienna."

That one statement meant more to me than Dewayne could ever possibly know. "Then you will," I replied. "But not now. This isn't the way to handle it."

Dewayne tilted his head, closed his eyes, and let out a heavy sigh. I couldn't imagine what he was thinking. All along I'd thought he'd known about Micah. This had to be a major shock for him. When he looked at me, I saw moisture in his eyes, and that alone won this man a place in my heart. For so long I had wanted someone to love Micah and want Micah as fiercely as I did.

"When can we talk?" he asked.

"I only work half days on Saturdays. I could leave Micah at day care a little longer, though I really hate the thought of that. Maybe it would be best to wait until he goes to bed tomorrow night."

Dewayne frowned. "Day care?"

"Yes," I replied defensively, not liking the tone of his voice. What did he expect me to do, take him to work with me?

"Can I watch him? I won't say anything. I swear. I just . . . I want to keep him while you work. We can talk after you get home. Maybe send him outside to play, and we can sit on the porch."

My instinct to protect wanted to refuse his request. I wasn't sure how much I trusted Dewayne not to say something to Micah about Dustin. But Dewayne wanted to be a part of his life. And I knew Micah wanted more family. He didn't ask anymore, but he wanted it. Lately he'd been talking about his dad a lot. He craved a male in his life.

"I need to leave at eight tomorrow," I told him before I could change my mind.

A relieved smile touched his lips. "I'll be here," he replied. Then he turned and walked back across the street. I didn't wait to see if he was going into his parents' home. I stepped quickly inside and closed the door behind me.

"You're gonna let him keep me tomorrow?" Micah asked, wide eyed.

Sighing, I took his hand. We walked over to the sofa and sat down. My legs were too tired from standing all day to squat. When I was at eye level with him, I held both his hands and looked him directly in the eyes. "I know I've acted weird around Dewayne. It's frightened you, and I understand that. But the truth is, I've known Dewayne since I was a kid. He's a good guy. There are things in our past that make me sad, but Dewayne never did anything wrong. I wouldn't leave you with someone I didn't trust. I think . . . I think you're gonna like Dewayne. Spending time with him will be fun. Much better than being stuck in day care on a Saturday."

Micah chewed on his bottom lip as his eyebrows drew

together. This was his thinking face. I let him take in what I'd said. It always took him a minute to make a decision about things. Finally he shrugged and smiled. "Okay. If you trust him, then I think it might be fun to have another man to hang out with."

I tried hard not to smile. Micah considered himself a man already. He had been the man of the house all his life.

He glanced over at the kitchen. "Think I could have some mac 'n' cheese?"

I pulled him into my arms and kissed him on the cheek. "I love you. You're my world," I told him. I'd been telling him that since I held him in my arms for the first time. It was the truth, and I never wanted him to forget it.

"Love you, too, Momma," he grunted in my tight embrace. "But you're squishing me."

Laughing, I let go of him, and he pointed to the kitchen. "I'd love some mac 'n' cheese," he reminded me.

I stood up and saluted him, making him giggle.

"Mac 'n' cheese, coming right up," I replied.

Micah was singing "Eye of the Tiger" loudly and off-key while he stood on a chair and fixed his Pop-Tart. I poured my coffee into a travel mug and tried to ignore the nervous knot in my stomach. I hadn't lied to Micah—I did trust Dewayne. I just wasn't sure that leaving him with an uncle he didn't know he had was such a good idea. Not until I was ready to talk to Micah about Dewayne and who the Falcos were to him. Upsetting Micah's world wasn't something I wanted to do.

He had been rolling with the punches since he was old enough to realize our life was always changing. We never knew where we would be next. Now that we had a house, I wanted him to have some security. Admitting to him that he had a family he didn't know about was something I was going to want to handle delicately.

"Think I should make Dewayne a Pop-Tart?" he asked, glancing over his shoulder at me.

"Hmm . . . Maybe you should wait and make sure he eats Pop-Tarts," I replied as I sipped my coffee and watched the cat clock on the wall. My mother loved cats. I wasn't a fan, really, but taking that clock down wasn't something I was ready to do. It reminded me of happier times.

A knock on the door threw those thoughts aside, and my nervous knot was back. I started for the door, but Micah jumped down from the chair and took off running. I let him go. Soon he'd be calling Dewayne "uncle" . . . maybe. If that was something Dewayne wanted. I knew I wanted it for Micah. Learning to share him, however, wasn't exactly going to be easy.

Micah threw open the door, and Dewayne was there filling the space in all his tattooed and pierced glory. Even at seven forty-five a.m. the man was breathtaking. His navy blue T-shirt that said FALCO CONSTRUCTION on the front hugged his body tightly. The size of his arms made a woman fantasize about wrapping her hands around them and jumping up into them. *No!* Dang it, what was I doing? I tore my gaze off Dewayne's body and didn't even let myself check out his legs in those jeans. And why were those leather bracelets on his arm sexy? The man could make anything sexy.

"I made a Pop-Tart," Micah announced. "You want one?"

Dewayne smiled brightly, and if I had been expected to speak, I wouldn't have been able to. I hadn't seen that smile in years. The devastating effect it had on me was still just as powerful.

"Never turn down a Pop-Tart," Dewayne replied, and Micah grabbed his hand.

"Then come on into the kitchen. I'll fix you one," he said, tugging Dewayne behind him.

"I'm glad I came on time, then."

Dewayne's expression of amazement as he looked at Micah made my heart squeeze. His dark brown eyes lifted to meet my gaze, and I managed to smile at him. But I didn't get emotional and weepy at the sight of him with Micah. I controlled myself. "You're better than on time. You're early," I said, trying to lighten the mood.

This was a big moment for Dewayne. Micah, too—he just didn't know it yet. After today I had no doubt that Dewayne would adore Micah.

"Didn't want to run you late. I'm trying to win the Saturday sitter gig," he said with a crooked grin.

The idea that Dewayne wanted to watch Micah every Saturday made me almost choke on my coffee. I hadn't expected that.

"Don't you work for your dad?" I asked, looking down at his shirt, then back up at him. Maybe I was assuming too much from the shirt. For all I knew he could be a lawyer. I highly doubted it with his dreadlocks, tattoos, and piercings, but I didn't know much about Dewayne. Not anymore.

"No, I run the company now. It's mine. Dad had to step down," he replied. "I don't work Saturdays."

Nodding, I held the coffee mug to my lips to give me a barrier. Not that it was much of one, but I didn't know what to think of Dewayne.

"You can have this Pop-Tart that I just made. I'll make another for me," Micah told him as he stood on the chair, holding out a paper plate with one Pop-Tart on it. "Milk's in the fridge. The good kind. Momma don't buy that watered-down stuff."

Grinning, I reached for my purse, then walked over to kiss Micah good-bye. "I'll see you after lunch. Be good for Dewayne, okay? I love you," I told him.

"Wait!" he called out, turning around on the chair and holding up his fist for me to bump. His big grin warmed everything inside me. I set my mug on the counter and tapped his fist with mine. "Dynamic Duo," we said in unison.

"Love you, Momma," he said, then turned back to the toaster.

"Love you more," I replied.

I picked up my mug, then glanced at Dewayne. He was watching me intently. I wasn't sure what he was thinking, but he was thinking about it hard.

"I need to go. You two have fun. I've left my work and cell number on the fridge if you need me," I told him, then headed for the door.

It wasn't easy to walk away, but I knew Micah needed this. And so did Dewayne.

DEWAYNE

Last night I stayed up most of the night letting one fear after another keep me awake. My biggest fear was for Micah's happiness. After watching Sienna with him this morning, I realized that what I'd thought was her being mental had actually been her being an overprotective mother. She loved that kid. And he loved her. That much was obvious.

But it still didn't explain why she hadn't told me about Micah. Why she hadn't contacted my parents. That was another thing—I hadn't told my parents yet. They were gonna see my truck over here today, and either my momma was gonna come knocking at the door, or I was gonna need to take Micah over there. Problem was, I was afraid my momma was gonna see what I'd missed the first time I looked at him.

Dustin had been her baby, so it would be easier for to make the connection when she saw his eyes and smile on Micah. She'd know. Immediately, she'd know. If I told her this was Sienna's boy, she would know. But I also knew she wouldn't say anything to Micah. She'd rail my ass later for not telling her as soon as I figured it out. But she wouldn't upset the kid.

It was probably best that I go ahead and deal with my mother before she came over here.

"Momma normally makes cinnamon rolls on Saturdays, but she's got to work on Saturdays now. She used to not have to work on Saturdays when we lived in Fort Worth. But our apartment there was so small. I like it better here. Just wish she didn't have to work," Micah said as he jumped down from the chair and pulled it behind him back to the table. I had a feeling I was going to find out a lot about his life today without even prying or asking questions. The kid just shared whatever was on his mind. No filter at all.

"She just has to work half the day. That's not too bad," I said, taking the seat across the table from him after pouring two glasses of whole milk. That must have been what the kid meant by "the good stuff." Dustin had always called whole milk "the good stuff." He complained that everything else was watered down. I liked that Sienna had passed that down to his son.

Unable to stop myself, I turned the conversation to his dad. I was curious as to what he knew about Dustin. "So, your dad was a good basketball player, huh?"

Micah swallowed his bite of Pop-Tart, and his eyes got big as he sat up on his knees in the chair. "He was the world's best," he said in all seriousness. "No one could beat him. I bet even LeBron James couldn't have beat my dad. Momma said he was a star." He stopped and took a drink of his milk, and then his eyes looked back up at me. "I think that's why God wanted him. Momma said God took him because he was such a good guy and he wanted him close to him. I think he wanted to make him a real star. You know, like the ones in the sky. There's this really big one that I used to see from my aunt Cathy's house in Fort Worth. I think that's my dad."

Damn. I couldn't take a deep breath. My chest constricted so hard it was painful. I didn't talk about Dustin. I had put his memory in a box and only touched it when I was too drunk to keep it hidden. Then I always let the anger take over.

But this kid . . . he kept Dustin's memory alive. I hadn't known I needed to hear someone talk about my brother like this, but listening to Micah eased the pain that never went away. The pain Dustin's death had left behind.

"You'll have to show me that star one night," I told him. If there was a God, then I was pretty damn sure that after hearing this little boy's words he'd make sure my brother was a star.

Micah nodded and dusted off his hands. He'd managed to finish his Pop-Tart in just a few bites. "I will. Come over at night and we'll go in my backyard and look for it. Momma said she'd help me find him, but we haven't had a chance this week. Been busy getting settled in," he explained. The kid talked like he was forty. It was pretty damn cute.

"Want to go over and meet my parents?" I asked him.

He jumped up and nodded enthusiastically.

It was better to go into this prepared than for my mother to walk over here and realize who Micah was on her own.

I stood up and held my hand out for Micah to take. "Let's go," I told him.

He slipped his little hand in mine. I was 100 percent sure Sienna would not be okay with this, but I had been so damn anxious to spend time with Micah that I hadn't thought through the fact that my folks would see my truck over here. When I'd pulled in this morning, I knew I had a problem. Pointing it out to Sienna would have meant her canceling our plans, and she would have taken Micah to day care. So I'd kept my mouth shut.

I knocked and decided to let Dad open it instead of just walking inside with Micah. Dad would help me handle Momma if she didn't react as calmly as I thought she would.

Dad opened the door and started to say something snide to me, but his gaze dropped to Micah. Recognition didn't dawn on his face. At least it wasn't just me who missed how much the kid looked like Dustin.

"This the drug lord?" Dad asked with a smirk.

Shit. The man had no boundaries. That wasn't funny.

"What's a drug lord?" Micah asked, looking up at me.

"Nothing you need to be concerned with. Ignore the old man. He thinks he's funny. He's not."

Micah nodded, then turned his gaze back to my dad. "I'm Micah. I live over there," he said, pointing to the house across the street.

Dad grinned down at him. "Is that so? Well, it's about time you got over here and introduced yourself."

"He and his momma, Sienna Roy, are living over there now. I'm watching him while Sienna works this morning, and I thought I'd bring him over to meet y'all. Think you can handle that . . . ? Can Momma handle that?" I informed him, hoping he understood what I was trying to say.

Dad's eyes swung back down to take in Micah, and I watched him as the realization slowly began to seep in. His hand tightened on the doorknob, and he stood there silently, unable to speak or stop looking at Micah. I cleared my throat.

"Can we come in now?" I asked, hoping he caught the warning in my tone.

It took him a moment, but then he stepped back and let us in. His eyes never left Micah. Maybe this had been a bad idea after all. Hell, I'd almost collapsed on my knees in Sienna's front yard when she'd told me. Was this good for my dad's heart? Shit.

"Who's here?" Momma called out just before she stepped around the corner and into the foyer. Her smile lit up her face when she saw it was me. "I didn't expect to see you today," she said. Then Micah moved beside me and her gaze dropped to him. "And you brought company." Her smile wavered then. Just like I had guessed. Momma saw her baby in Micah's little face.

"Momma, this is Micah. He lives across the street." I couldn't bring myself to tell her who he was just yet. Even if she saw the resemblance, I knew she wouldn't guess correctly unless she knew his mother's name.

She didn't take her eyes off Micah as she walked into the room. A range of emotions danced across her face, the last one being complete awe. Stopping in front of him, she held out her hand, and her smile was brighter than I had seen it in a long time. "Hello, Micah. I'm Tabby Falco, but you can call me Mama T, like the rest of the boys around here do."

Micah held up his little hand and slipped it in hers. "I like the name Mama T. And where are the other boys?"

My mother seemed to be soaking up everything he said

and did. "Well, those boys are all big now, just like my boy is," she said, nodding at me. "So they are all over the place."

Micah glanced back at me. "Oh well, that's okay. I like Dewayne. Except when he made my momma cry. I didn't like him then, but Momma said that it was a misunderstanding and that I shouldn't be mad at him. So I ain't."

Shit! The kid just said whatever the hell . . .

"Dewayne? You made his mother cry?" Momma asked me, her eyebrows raised. She had a very concerned look on her face.

"Like he said, it was a misunderstanding," I assured her, hoping the kid didn't say anything else about his momma.

I glanced over at Dad, who was watching Micah with the same look of wonder that I had felt when I'd realized who he was. Momma didn't know yet, and I decided that if Dad didn't tell her, then maybe I should wait until later, when Micah wasn't around.

"I have chocolate chip cookies and apple pie in my kitchen, fresh outta the oven. You want some?" she asked Micah, squeezing his hand in hers.

He nodded vigorously. "Yes, ma'am, I do. I love both those things."

Momma didn't even look at Dad or me. Micah had her undivided attention. "Well, it's a good thing you moved in across the street, then. Because I need someone to eat all these sweets I bake."

Micah walked away, still holding her hand. "I like sweets. I'll eat 'em," he assured her.

I waited until they were in the kitchen and I heard Micah rattling on about superheroes needing lots of cookies before looking at Dad.

He shook his head and let out a heavy sigh. "Wow. He looks just like him. Just like him," he said, before turning his gaze toward me. I saw the hope there. The feeling that there was something of Dustin's to hold on to. I understood because I was feeling it too.

"I wasn't sure telling Momma in front of him was a good idea once I got over here. Changed my mind."

Dad nodded. "Yeah. She sees Dustin in him. She just doesn't realize exactly how much of Dustin she's seeing. She thinks it's just a coincidental resemblance, and she's already in love with the kid. He's gonna be good for her. I just"—he paused and glanced back at the house across the street—"I can't figure out why she kept him from us. We loved that girl. She was like our own. Why would she not let us be a part of his life?"

I wasn't sure, exactly, but I knew she thought we didn't want him and didn't care to know him. That was something I was going to figure out today. "I'm talking with her later. She thought I knew who Micah was and thought I'd chosen not to be a part of his life. Not sure how that works, since I didn't know where the fuck she was all these years. No one did."

Dad rubbed his stubbled jaw and shook his head. "Your momma is gonna want answers. So let's wait until you get them before we tell her."

I nodded. I was in complete agreement.

Chapter Five

SIENNA

My morning went fast. Three cut-and-styles, one highlight, and one root touch-up. All of them were last-minute walk-ins who couldn't get an appointment with their regular stylist. Right now that was what I had to work with, and I was okay with that. Hillary was even telling people we accepted walk-ins, for my benefit.

The only employee other than Hillary who was working today was Gretchen. This was my second time working with her, and she was very loud and chatty. She laughed a lot too. And she had a ton of male clients. The tight leather pants she was so fond of seemed to be popular with the men.

"I heard you talking to your son earlier on the phone. You mentioned Dewayne," Hillary said as she sauntered back into the room in spiked heels. How that woman wore those heels and stood on her feet all day was beyond me.

I nodded, not sure why she was bringing up the short conversation I'd had with Micah an hour ago to make sure everything was okay. He'd been outside throwing the football around with Dewayne and had been ready to get off the phone with me and go back to having fun.

"Was it Falco you were talking about? Seeing as how you knew Amanda Hardy when she came in, and then I heard Dewayne's name, and since he's one of Preston's friends I thought maybe you knew Dewayne, too."

Still wasn't sure why this mattered. "Yeah, it was Dewayne Falco. He's watching Micah for me today."

Hillary studied me a moment, and then a small grin tugged on her lips. "You're not messing around with Dewayne, are you? He ain't a sticking-around kind of guy. He's more of a several-girls-a-week kind of guy."

I already knew this. Dewayne had always been a player. However, I wasn't interested in Dewayne for any reason other than to be a part of Micah's life. Micah needed a man in his life, and his uncle would be his only chance to have that.

"You seeing Dewayne Falco?" Gretchen asked, swinging her head around and sending her dark curls bouncing. "That boy can . . . do it well. You know what I mean. Damn near ruined me for anyone else. I had to work him out of my system."

Hillary gave me a pointed look as if to say, *See what I mean?*

I was trying to push all thoughts of Dewayne and Gretchen doing it well out of my head. Not a mental image I needed, even though I was sure Dewayne's naked ass was a lovely sight to behold.

"I swear, if he came sniffing around again, I'd give him a go and deal with the withdrawal later. He's just that good."

Okay, I'd had enough of Gretchen's sexfest with Dewayne. "He's an old friend. He was my high school boyfriend's older brother. Nothing more. He's just helping me out by watching Micah." I finished cleaning up my station as I talked. I didn't want either of their prying eyes on me, but I could feel them burning a hole in my head.

"You dated his younger brother? The one who was in the accident?"

Crap. Not what I wanted to talk about. I simply nodded and kept busy. I wasn't allowing Dustin to become a topic of conversation.

Gretchen seemed to get that, so she didn't pry and she shut up. Relieved, I put the broom away and grabbed my phone to see if I had a text from Micah. Normally, he texted me several times when he was staying with someone. He hadn't texted me at all today. Dewayne must've been entertaining him.

Gretchen changed the subject to her need for a pedicure and the date she had tonight with some guy named Green.

Anyone with the name Green sounded unstable, but I didn't say anything. Gretchen had a different guy every weekend, mostly her customers from the salon.

"Tomorrow night is girls' night. When are you coming out with us, Sienna?" Hillary asked as she looked at me in the mirror she was standing in front of to fix her hair.

"I can't leave Micah at night," I said by way of explanation. I would never be going out with them. I was positive their going out meant drinking and men. I didn't have time for either.

"Can't you get a sitter?" Gretchen asked.

It was odd how Gretchen was two years older than me but acted much younger. She seemed like she never had any real worries and was always partying and going out. I shook my head. "I don't know anyone I can leave Micah with and feel comfortable. I don't think Dewayne would be open to watching him on a weekend night. He has his own social life to see to."

"My younger sister is a sitter. She has been to classes and everything to learn CPR and handle all those emergency situations. She's only seventeen, but she's good at it. Makes good money and has several regulars who have come to trust her and call on her." Hillary's seventeen-year-old sister was the same age I was when I'd had to grow up fast. I didn't doubt her because of her age, but I wasn't sure I was ready to leave Micah with a stranger.

"I'll think about it," I said, not wanting to insult Hillary.

She nodded. "I understand. But she would gladly come spend some time with you and Micah so you can get to know her. She learned that it was better for the kids and parents if she did that first before sitting for them."

Hillary's sister would also require money. From the sound of her professionalism with the whole sitting thing, she probably charged more than I could pay. I didn't want to spend our money on me going out when Micah needed so many things. I had his future to think about.

"Money's tight right now. Maybe when it isn't so tight, I'll give her a call," I said, hoping this was enough to get Hillary to stop pressing the issue.

She shrugged. "Just let me know when you think you're ready. I'll hook you up."

I thanked her and checked my phone again for a text.

Still nothing.

DEWAYNE

The kid could throw a football. For five years old, he had an impressive arm. He was obsessed with basketball, but he had a talent that was going untapped. I caught the next ball he hurled at me and watched as he grinned and blew his fingers as if they were on fire. It was something my brother would have done.

Instead of my chest hurting with the memory of a little boy

who looked almost exactly like this one, strutting around the basketball court like he was king, I felt an empty place inside me being filled. Micah was so much like Dustin that I had fallen in love with him in less than six hours.

My dad hadn't been able to take his eyes off Micah either. Once the shock wore off, he'd sat down beside his grandson and asked him so many things. And when Micah told him that he was a basketball fan and that he was going to be the best, Dad beamed like I hadn't seen him do in six years. Micah also mentioned that his dad had been the world's best basketball player. It had been pure luck that Momma had gone back into the kitchen just when he mentioned his father.

But *my* father had heard him. Seeing his eyes mist over with bittersweet tears had gotten to me. I'd needed to get the kid out of there. My momma had to be told gently, and when Micah wasn't around to see her reaction. I had explained that Micah and I had some things to do, and we'd said our good-byes. Momma had made Micah promise to come visit again soon, and my dad had kissed the top of his head. He hadn't been able to help himself.

"Momma's home!" Micah cheered and dropped the ball he had just caught, then took off running to meet Sienna as she got out of her beat-to-shit car. The boy loved his mother. She must have raised him without her parents' help, because Micah said he didn't have grandparents. He said he had an aunt Cathy they used to live with in Fort Worth. That was it. He hadn't had anyone else to talk about.

"Hey, Ace." Sienna's voice caught my attention, and I took my eyes off Micah to see the woman he was throwing himself at and latching on to. Her long hair wasn't up like it had been earlier today. She had pulled it loose and let it hang down her back. All that red hair. Damn. I had to remember who she was and how off-limits that was. The way she looked wasn't something I could focus on. Hooking up for a casual fuck with Sienna Roy was never gonna happen. She was the mother of my nephew.

And I didn't do anything more than a casual fuck. Ever.

Sienna was responsibility. And she was mine already, even if she didn't know it yet. I would help take care of her and Micah, but adding sex to that mix was completely against the rules. It would fuck up everything. I had to be a part of Micah's life. That was what was important. Not the fact that his momma had legs that didn't stop, and a face . . . damn, that face. Those motherfucking gorgeous eyes, and her lips. Jesus, I had to forget this shit. She was Micah's mom. That was it.

"Did y'all have a good morning?" Sienna asked.

I tore my eyes off her and all that perfection and looked at Micah. I needed to regroup. Dealing with this woman wasn't gonna be easy if I didn't stop imagining her naked and in my bed. I didn't put women in my bed. Ever. Fuck that.

"It was awesome! Mama T gave me chocolate chip cookies *and* apple pie. And she had real milk like us, and she said I could come eat anytime I wanted to."

The color drained from Sienna's face as she looked from her son to me. I had to explain why I'd taken him over there. It wasn't to undermine her but to deal with it before my mother came over here and figured shit out the wrong way. Plus, Micah had no idea who my parents were to him.

"He met my parents. That's all," I said, hoping she read the unspoken words from the pointed look on my face.

She swallowed and took a deep breath, then turned her gaze back to her son. "Well, now it's my time to talk to Dewayne about things. I need you to go play in your room with all those toys you have while we talk, okay?" she said, with a tremor in her voice that didn't go unnoticed by the kid. He frowned, and his happy smile turned to a warning glare as he looked at me. He was a little thing, but no one had told him that. He was more than ready to take care of his momma if he needed to. Dustin would have been so damn proud of that boy.

"Don't make my momma cry" was his simple demand.

"It's okay, baby. I promise. We just have to talk about good stuff, like Dewayne watching you again and maybe you visiting Tab . . . Mama T again. Okay?"

Micah looked back at her and studied her face before nodding, but he didn't look real sure. Then he wrapped his arms around her neck and squeezed tightly before letting her go. He then turned and ran to the door.

When the screen door closed behind him, Sienna turned to look at me. "You took him over there without asking me."

I had been prepared for those to be the first words out of her mouth. "They missed the first five years of his life, Sienna. Dustin was their baby. Their golden boy. They have mourned him for the past six years. It wasn't fair that all this time they could have had a part of Dustin that they didn't even know about."

Sienna's back went stiff, and she raised her chin in a defensive pose. Damn, she was even more gorgeous when fire was flashing in her eyes. "I sent them photos of him for two years. I begged your mother for help when I realized my parents were disowning me if I kept the baby. Nothing," she said. "*Nothing*. I got nothing from your mother. She never once replied. I grew up in that house." Sienna pointed to my parents' house. "It was my second home. I loved those people, and then, when I needed them most, when Dustin's child needed them, they turned their back on me too. You have no idea how that felt. No idea."

I heard the words she was saying, but I knew for a fact that my parents had known nothing about Micah. My mother would have been in Fort Worth by Sienna's side if she'd known. Something was off here.

"You know Momma, Sienna. She'd have been there if she knew. She would have been there every motherfucking step of the way. Momma loved Dustin, and she loved you. Micah would have been the center of her world."

Sienna was shaking her head. "No, she wouldn't, because she wasn't. I see that she still lives at the same address, Dewayne. She hasn't moved. I sent her letters. More than I can count. Not once did she respond. Not once."

This wasn't right. I just didn't have an answer other than that my mother didn't know about Micah. She couldn't. She would have wanted that baby. She would have made sure Sienna had everything she needed.

"We need to talk to Momma. Something isn't right. She doesn't know, Sienna. Hell, my father almost passed out when he figured it out. Momma still doesn't know who he is, but when I told Dad who Micah's mother was, he saw Dustin in the boy immediately. He wouldn't move from his side from that moment on. He asked him questions and he watched him with complete fascination. When we left, he kissed his head. *My dad kissed Micah's head*. My dad isn't affectionate. You know that. So tell me you believe they knew about Micah and ignored him."

Sienna stood there, and then, instead of arguing, she burst into tears. Shit! Micah was gonna be so damn pissed at me.

Chapter Six

SIENNA

They wanted him. His dad had kissed Micah's head. For years I had longed for Micah to have family. Grandparents who loved him. Someone other than just me and Aunt Cathy. This was all too much. I had sent those letters to Tabby. Was it possible she hadn't received them? So many of them?

"Fuck, Sienna. Please don't cry. Micah will blame me," Dewayne said, sounding panicked. The fact that Dewayne Falco was worried about a five-year-old boy being mad at him made me cry harder. He wanted Micah to like him. He wanted to be a part of Micah's life too. I hadn't expected this at all. I had been terrified to return to Sea Breeze.

But this . . . I hadn't needed to be scared of this. I had been worried about Micah being hurt. But instead Micah got others who love him. The fear of what would happen to him if I died wasn't as heavy anymore. I had always lived with that constant terror. Micah was going to have a family. One bigger than just me. A group of people who he could trust to be there for him.

"I sent letters . . . pictures," I said, mostly for my benefit, to remind myself I had tried to tell her . . . to tell them.

Dewayne nodded. "I believe you. I do. I just know my momma didn't get them."

That was the Tabby Falco I remembered. The one who Dewayne insisted would have been there if she'd known. The one who wouldn't have let me live in Fort Worth in a house with an aunt who didn't force me to give up my baby, but who also didn't approve of a pregnant teen. She had given me a roof over my head and a ride when I needed it, but she hadn't been warm and kind.

I wiped at my now-wet face and took a deep breath to calm myself. Dewayne was right. Micah wouldn't understand my tears, and he'd be upset. He didn't like seeing me cry. I think it scared him.

"If they want to be a part of Micah's life, I want that for him. He needs family. He wants it." I swallowed and concentrated on not breaking down again when I said this to Dewayne. "He has always wondered where his grandparents were. Other kids had them, and he didn't understand why all he had was a momma, and an aunt who he wasn't very close to. She was more like a landlord."

Dewayne looked pained. "They're gonna adore the kid. He will have the best damn grandparents on earth. Just give them a chance. If you can do that, you may save them both. Micah is what they need. He'll bring back the joy that Dustin took with him."

Micah and I needed to talk first. "Give me time to help him understand. And then I'll call you and let you know we're ready. But I need to make sure that your mother didn't get those letters. Because I sent them . . . and if she got them and . . ." I trailed off. I hated saying to her son that she could have known about Micah and hid it from Dewayne and his father. I'd sent those letters. They couldn't have just vanished.

"She didn't get them. How did you send them? Did you mail them from your aunt's?"

I nodded. I had put them in the mailbox in the mornings.

"Would your aunt have taken them?"

No. Why would Aunt Cathy take them? She didn't want us there with her. She was taking us in because she didn't want us on the streets. I shook my head. "I can't imagine she would have."

Dewayne frowned. He didn't look convinced. "Momma didn't get them. Something must have happened to them. It's possible someone intercepted them."

I hoped he was right. Because more than anything, I wanted the Falcos to be a part of Micah's life. I wanted him to know the people who were a part of his father. I wanted him to see pictures of his father growing up. All those things. I wanted them for him.

"You find out if she ever received those letters, and then I'll talk to Micah. I need to know they want this first."

Dewayne nodded and shoved his hands in his front pockets. "I'll talk to Momma and let you know as soon as possible. But can we go ahead and confirm that I'm hanging out with Micah on Saturday mornings while you work? I want that time."

Micah needed that, and it would save me money. I nodded. "Yes. That's good. If you can't one Saturday, just let me know at least a week in advance so I can make other arrangements."

Dewayne grinned. "When you tell those people across the street that Micah is Dustin's son, you will have free child care whenever you want it."

Something else I wasn't used to.

We said our good-byes, and I watched as Dewayne turned and headed for his truck. I may have watched his ass as he made his way to the truck, but that was my secret.

"What did he want?" Micah asked the moment I walked inside. He was sitting on the sofa with his arms crossed over his chest and his feet dangling because they couldn't touch the floor yet.

"You were supposed to be playing in your room," I reminded him as I made my way over to sit down beside my little man.

"I was watching out for you," he said simply.

I reached over, pulled him against my side, and hugged him to me. It had been just us for so long. This past year he had started acting like he was the one protecting me instead of the other way around. A month ago he had asked me who kept me safe since I didn't have a husband to do it. I informed him that I kept me and him safe. I assured him I was very good at it.

He'd changed that day. I was seeing it more and more every day. It was as if he'd realized I needed someone to take care of me, and he was doing that job. Sweet little boy of mine. I kissed his head and inhaled his outdoor smell.

"Did you enjoy your day?" I asked him.

He nodded slowly. "Yeah, but if Dewayne was mean to you, then I don't want him to come back."

He was about to have a whole new world opened up to him. One that would change his life. I squeezed him. "Dewayne wasn't mean to me. Dewayne wants what I want. He wants you safe and happy."

Micah leaned back and looked up at me. I could see the confusion in his little face. He wasn't sure what I was saying, and the little bit of hope in those eyes of his just about undid me. He didn't want me to know how much he wanted a man in his life, but I knew it and understood it.

It wasn't time to tell him just how much Dewayne wanted him in his life and why. I still needed to know that Tabby Falco hadn't gotten those letters. I had to be sure she was unaware of

Micah. Because as much as Dewayne believed his mother would never do this, I knew I had sent her letters. They had to have gone somewhere.

"Will Dewayne come back again one day to play?"

He wanted Dewayne to come back. It was in his hopeful expression. I was glad he had enjoyed his time with Dewayne. "Yes. Every Saturday morning Dewayne wants to hang out with you while I work."

A bright smile lit up his face. "He does?"

I nodded, and Micah punched his fist into the air with a cheer and jumped down from the sofa. I watched as he ran off to his room, signaling the end of our conversation. Smiling, I stood up and went to fix myself a sandwich.

"You want lunch?" I asked him.

"Mac 'n' cheese," he called back.

"You're gonna turn into mac 'n' cheese," I replied.

"Good! Then I'll eat myself."

Shaking my head, I laughed and fixed my son some mac 'n' cheese.

DEWAYNE

If I went home tonight, I'd only think about shit. So I went out to Live Bay, where I knew I'd have friends. People to distract me. It was where some of us always showed up on weekends. Even my married-with-kids friends.

I sat back with a beer and watched as Krit Corbin sang while eye-fucking his girlfriend. It was like some strange turn in the universe. When Preston Drake had fallen in love with our best friend's little sister, I'd thought he had lost his ever-loving mind. Now the Sea Breeze man whore and lead singer of Jackdown was completely fucked over a girl. The world was going to shit.

"I love watching him watch her," said Trisha, Krit's older sister and Rock's wife. Rock had also been one of my best friends since elementary school. Trisha had been a part of our lives since Rock had locked himself around her when we were seventeen. I had once made the mistake of asking if she had a magic pussy. Rock had leveled my ass in one swing. I hadn't even seen it coming.

I didn't talk about Trisha's pussy again. Lesson learned.

"He's fucking whipped," I said before taking another swig of beer. I had a good thirty pounds of muscle on Krit, though I'd seen his ass go crazy once when he thought Blythe had left him. So I wasn't talking about her pussy in front of him. Dude would lose his shit, and I didn't have that kind of energy.

"You're so jaded," said Trisha, who was sitting on her husband's lap.

"Honest, sweetheart; I'm just brutally honest."

Trisha rolled her eyes. "One day, Dewayne Falco, you will fall, and when you do I'm gonna enjoy the hell out of watching it."

She was wrong about that, but I didn't want to argue. I was trying not to smoke. If that shit did kill people, then I needed to save a few years. I had a nephew who needed me now. I hadn't had that before. But motherfuck did I want a cigarette.

"We're here! Sorry we're late. Bliss was not in the mood to stay with a sitter tonight. Cage had to rock her to sleep first," Eva York said as she sat her beautiful ass down on a stool beside me. She slapped my knee. "Hey, you," she said with the smile that had been Cage York's downfall. He'd taken one look at Eva, and the player once known as Cage York had transformed. Eva had that magic pussy too. Only fucking explanation for that shit. Cage was a daddy now, and he was happy about it. You asked him about his baby girl and his face would go all soft and dreamy. Crazy shits. All of them.

I leaned over toward Eva and winked. "Just waiting on you to show up, sugar," I told her in a low voice, just to piss Cage off. Dude was funny as shit when he went territorial on Eva's hot ass.

"Fuck you, Dewayne," Cage growled, and he pulled Eva onto his leg and nuzzled her neck as if they were horny and dating instead of married and parents.

"Amanda called and said she had the kids," Eva said, giggling from Cage's attention.

Trisha nodded. "Yep. Preston wanted the kids tonight, so we took them over there and came to hear Krit. I thought I might get to visit with Blythe, too, but he won't let her out here. He's keeping her back there with him. It's why he keeps singing to someone offstage. He rarely takes his eyes off her." The pleased sound in Trisha's voice was hard to miss.

"I love that. They are adorable," Eva said, looking up at the stage and at Krit Corbin singing to the woman no one could see offstage.

Cage slipped his hand over Eva's stomach, and she laughed and tried to move away from his groping. He was getting a little carried away, which was normal.

"I'm all about watching, but I don't know if that's legal. Might wanna pour some cold water on him," I said with a smirk.

Cage shot me an annoyed glare. "Jealous, Falco?"

I glanced over at the blonde who had been sending me flirty signals all night. She wasn't dressed in much, and she had that look in her eyes. She was at the beach to party.

I crooked my finger at her, and that was all it took. She bounced her perky little ass over to me.

"Hey, sugar, you're trying to get my attention pretty damn hard," I said, sliding a hand around her waist. She snuggled up to me, and I could smell the beer on her breath. She was nice and lubed up. I cut my eyes at Cage. "New pussy every damn night," I whispered to him over the top of her head, then pulled her face to mine and took a taste.

"One day, Dewayne. One day," Trisha said, but I ignored her taunting and enjoyed the willing young blonde in my arms. Her curves were nice. Her ass wasn't as plump as I liked—I grabbed it with one of my hands—but she would do.

"How old are you?" I asked before taking a bite of her neck.

"Nineteen," she breathed. She looked nineteen and she felt nineteen. I'd require an ID before I stuck my dick in her, but I believed her. That was enough for now.

"You good with that mouth?" I asked her, slipping my hand farther over her ass until my fingers touched her crotch. The whoosh of breath that came out of her told me she was ready.

"I can be good at anything you want me to be," she said teasingly.

I liked this one. "Then sit that sweet ass on my leg and let me visit with my friends," I told her. As I reached for my beer she did exactly as I told her. She was like all of them, the beauties who came to the beach looking for a good time. A good time they could leave behind here in Sea Breeze once they went back to their lives. I was more than happy to give them a memory to take back with them.

I had just two rules: never at my place—I didn't fuck them at my place—and never overnight. We fucked, and if it was good, we fucked a couple of times. Then I left. It was over. I didn't even need their names.

Relationships took too much thought. They took time. They took a shitload of stuff I didn't want to give. Sure, I got why each of my friends had fallen under his woman's spell. They each picked beauties with something more than a nice pair of tits. They had the whole package, and I was happy for them. I just didn't fucking want to be them.

"You hear that, Dewayne? I expected a snide comment," Rock said, breaking into my thoughts. My hand had made its way between the blonde's legs, and I was busy working her up while I made her sit here.

"Jess is pregnant," Trisha said with a look of pride.

Jess was Rock's cousin, and once she'd been one sweet little piece of tail. Then she'd run off with a rock star's brother. He'd fallen in love with her and taken her from her life here and changed everything for her. I wouldn't admit it, but I was happy for her. She had a good heart, and I used to worry she was going to end up giving it to Krit, who would never be faithful to her. But he wasn't owned by her, and I didn't think he could be faithful—until he'd met Blythe.

"Jess as a momma," I said, then laughed. That was hard to picture. The girl had the body of a fucking porn star, and before Jason Stone had walked into her life, she'd used that body to bring men to their knees.

The girl in my lap let out a soft moan, and I remembered I had my hand up her skirt, playing around. I better get her out to the truck. That was as far as we were gonna make it. I wasn't in the mood to go back to this one's hotel room.

"Looks like I got to go put out a fire. I'll see y'all later," I said, standing up. I took the girl by the hips and moved her through the crowd.

"You wet, sugar?" I asked as I pushed her out the door and into the cool night air.

She nodded and looked up at me with hooded eyes. Problem was, I wasn't in the mood to fuck. I hadn't fucked in two weeks. Not since I'd been informed that I had a nephew. It had screwed with my head, and I couldn't focus on anything else. Not even the very willing woman in my arms. I'd worked her up, though, and I needed to fix that.

"My truck," I told her, and led her back there and pushed her up against it, then slipped my hands back up the tiny skirt she was wearing and fingered her very wet and hot cunt while she bucked against my hand.

This should have been turning me on. Having one so willing to take me. But it wasn't. Not in the least. I felt like I was doing a job. Fuck this. I needed her to come so I could go home and get a shower.

"Come for me, sugar. Come all over my hand," I said in her ear, knowing words could push a horny woman over the edge. Sure enough, that's all it took. She trembled and cried out as she held on to my arms. When I was sure she was done, I pulled my hand out, then wiped it casually on her skirt. I didn't want her scent on me. I needed the damn hand sanitizer in my truck.

She looked up at me with dreamy eyes. At least she'd gotten some pleasure out of it. I, however, was done for the night. "Go on back in, sugar. I'll watch you from here to make sure you make it in safe."

Her pleased smile slowly turned into a frown as she stared up at me. "What about you?"

What about me? I'd given her a fucking orgasm and let her come all over my damn hand. I was going home. "I'm headed home. You head on back inside and find your friends," I told her, then gave her a gentle push toward the door. She stumbled, then glanced back at me with a frustrated scowl.

"Didn't promise you a fuck, babe. You were hot and bothered, and I gave you a release. I'm not interested in more. Go on along now," I told her.

That seemed to be enough of a slap to her ego. Her back snapped straight, and she swung her head around and stalked off.

Good. Now I could go home and shower her off me.

Chapter Seven

SIENNA

I hadn't told Micah about the Falcos tonight. I still needed to make sure Tabby Falco hadn't received those letters. We had watched *Star Wars: Episode III* (which was my favorite) and eaten two bags of popcorn. When I'd tucked him into bed, he hadn't even stirred. He'd had a long day.

After my long soak in the tub I crawled into bed. It was nice to be back in my bed. I had good memories of home. Before . . . before I'd lost Dustin. I didn't let myself think about the bad. I didn't let myself wonder why Dustin had gotten drunk and driven his car into a tree only hours after we had had sex in that exact same car. Whenever he'd driven me, he had been so careful. He was always taking care of me. Protecting me.

My phone started ringing. I reached over and grabbed it,

surprised to see Dewayne's name on the screen. Why would he be calling me at midnight on a Saturday?

"Hello?" I said, almost expecting this to be a pocket dial.

"Hey." Dewayne's deep voice came over the line, and my lady parts woke up with that one word. Crap! What was wrong with me? I hadn't had sex in . . . well . . . since Dustin. And what I remembered from sex was not good. The pleasure I could bring myself in bed at night all alone wasn't a feeling I'd ever experienced with Dustin.

"I want to talk to my mom tomorrow about the letters. Did you tell Micah?"

He was calling me at midnight on a Saturday to ask about Micah. Didn't Dewayne have a date? He always had a chick on his arm.

"No. I'm not talking to him until I know what happened to those letters. I don't want him knowing about y'all unless he will be accepted. He's too little to understand anything else."

Dewayne let out a sigh. "I told you already. My momma didn't get those letters. But even if she did, I want Micah in my life. He's my little brother's kid. I want him."

So he wanted Micah to know who he was. Could I explain that without explaining about the rest of the Falcos?

"I need to know how your mother feels first. Micah is my number one concern. I won't let him get hurt."

"Me neither," Dewayne replied.

Good. At least he wasn't willing to play with Micah's emotions.

"I'll see you tomorrow. I'll probably be right behind my momma while she's knocking on your door—or possibly barging in. Once she knows, you won't be able to keep her away from him."

He had no idea how much I hoped that was true.

"You talk to her. I'll wait" was my only response.

Dewayne was quiet for a moment, and I wasn't sure if he had hung up or not.

"Good night, Sienna," he finally said, and the way his sexy, warm voice curled around my name made me shiver. Dammit.

"Good night," I replied, then hung up. Laying the phone down beside me, I slipped a hand under the covers and into the front of my lace panties. All I needed was the memory of Dewayne's deep voice while I eased the ache he inspired.

This wasn't the first time I'd fantasized about Dewayne. For so long I'd felt guilty that it was him and not Dustin I used as inspiration. But I'd finally resigned myself to the fact that I'd never felt any pleasure with Dustin. Dewayne was a fantasy, and that was all this was. Something that wasn't real.

I slid my fingers inside, closed my eyes, and let Dewayne's body take shape in my mind. His sexy grin and those arms. Lord, those arms were something else. Wrapping my hands around them as they flexed and he moved inside me . . . My body trembled at the thought. The beautiful thing about using

Dewayne to satisfy my need was that the idea of him touching me and being inside me set my body on fire.

It was so easy to forget that he wasn't there. That he wasn't touching me. The gleam in his eyes when he looked at me sometimes made me think he thought about this too.

But it could never happen. I'd get hurt. I knew that. Still, the thought of having him on top of me, rocking his hips as he moved in and out of my very neglected body, made me ache. Just once I wanted to know how it felt to be loved by Dewayne Falco.

"Momma? Wake up!" Micah's voice broke into my dreams, and I opened my eyes, only to immediately close them again. The sunlight was pouring into the room and blinding me. "I know you like to sleep late on Sundays, but there's someone knocking at the door."

Micah's words sank in, and I sat up in bed and rubbed my eyes before slowly opening them and looking down at him.

"Sounds like Dewayne and Mama T arguing outside, but you said not to open the door without you, so I didn't. I came and got you."

Oh crap! I threw my legs over the bed and reached for the silk wrap Janell had given me for Christmas last year. I needed to get dressed, but the knocking and voices were getting louder. I had to go out there and deal with them. Now. Before Micah heard something he didn't need to hear.

I tied the belt around my waist and ran my hand through my hair, then bent down to look Micah in the eyes. "You and I have something to talk about later. It's about a good thing. But first I need to go outside and talk to them, and I need you to stay in your room and play like you were doing before they knocked, okay?"

He nodded, but the frown on his face told me he didn't like that he wasn't going with me. I kissed his forehead, then hurried to the door before Tabby Falco broke it down.

Glancing back, I saw Micah go into his room, and I took that moment to open the door and step outside on the porch with a red-eyed Tabby Falco; her husband, Dave; and of course Dewayne.

I didn't let myself think about the look in Dewayne's eyes as he took in my appearance. I was a mess, with bed head and no makeup. But I wasn't out here to impress Dewayne. I wouldn't think about that.

"I never got a letter. Not one letter, Sienna Roy! If I had gotten a letter, I'd have come after you and my grandbaby. What were your parents thinking? You were a kid! A baby having a baby, and they left you! I just don't understand it. And that precious boy who looks so much like my Dustin. . . ." She choked up, covered her mouth, and sobbed. Dave pulled her against his chest.

"Please, I know this is a lot. And I know you're upset, I can see that. And as thankful as I am that you do want him, I don't want him hearing this. He needs me to explain it and talk to him first. This would be too traumatic for him."

"She's right, Momma. You gotta calm down," Dewayne added.

I wouldn't look at him. I couldn't. I kept my focus on Tabby. She nodded, then dropped her hand from her mouth and looked up at me. She had always been a tiny woman, which was so weird in contrast to her huge sons. Then again, Dave Falco was a massive man.

"Look at you," she said in a whisper. "You're all grown up and beautiful." The sincere smile on her face made me tear up, and I blinked back the tears burning my eyes. I wouldn't cry. I had Micah to think about. She looked back at Dewayne. "She is much more than average, Dewayne Falco! Are you blind?"

That hurt so much more than it should have.

DEWAYNE

Motherfucking hell. My mother had no damn filter on her mouth. Maybe that was where the kid got it from. The color on Sienna's cheeks at my mother's words told me Momma had seriously embarrassed her. *Fuck!*

Sienna had come out of the house in nothing but that short silk wrap and her hair looking like she'd been properly fucked, and my imagination went to just that. To what it would be like to have those legs of hers wrapped around me and that gorgeous face of hers in the throes of an orgasm. The idea of anyone else seeing her like this pissed me off. I'd moved to the side so the view of her was blocked from anyone driving down the road or looking out their windows. Did she not realize she looked like a walking fantasy?

Then my mother had gone and told her I'd said she was average. Damn, that sucked. I didn't want her thinking I was attracted to her, because that would complicate things, but I also didn't like her thinking I was talking bad about her. I wanted her to like me. I wanted to be around Micah as much as possible.

"She's absolutely beautiful. You have to beat those men off with a stick, don't you, honey?" my mother continued with her praise of Sienna. She was right, of course, but what was I supposed to say now? I already looked like a douchebag. I kept my mouth shut.

"I, uh, I . . . Thank you," she said with an unsure, forced smile.

"How are you still single? You should have a man taking care of you," my mother said.

The pink on Sienna's fair cheeks only got brighter. "I don't date. I have Micah to think of first."

Shit. She was a good mom. I had known a lot of single moms, and none of them sacrificed a social life because of their kid.

"But you're young, and Micah needs a man. Don't worry about that. He's gonna have his uncle Dewayne and his grandpa Dave there for him. Maybe you can think of spending some time with a man soon. It's a shame for a beauty like you to live life alone. Dustin wouldn't have wanted that."

Sienna swallowed nervously. "It's okay. I'm happy with it being just me and Micah."

Momma waved her hand. "Nonsense. You have us now, and we'll make sure you have a life, too. Being a momma is the most important job you can have, but you have to think about you, too. Enough of that for now." She walked up and pulled Sienna into her arms and held her tightly. "You're here. And you have Dustin's boy," Momma said, choking up again. "I'm so happy. I'm just so happy."

Sienna's eyes misted over as she looked up at me briefly, then over at my dad, and she smiled. "I sent letters," she said, feeling the need to defend herself.

Momma nodded and pulled back. "I believe you did. But I didn't get them. I think you might want to give that aunt of yours a call. That's the only explanation I got. But those letters never made it to me."

Sienna nodded. "Okay. I, uh . . . I need time with Micah. When he's ready, we'll come over for a visit. He enjoyed his last visit over there. He's a fan of cookies," she said, smiling so sweetly.

My mother had always loved Sienna Roy, and she'd encouraged Dustin's relationship with her, but right now I realized that the love she'd had for Sienna just multiplied by a thousand because Sienna had brought Dustin's child into the world. She'd given my momma a part of her son back.

Which was something I'd never been able to do.

Dad finally spoke up, tugging on my mother's arm. "Let's go back over to the house and let them talk." She nodded, but she looked longingly at the door to the house, knowing her grandson was in there.

"Our door is always open, Sienna," my dad told her.

She sniffed and smiled. "Thank you." The look on her face told me just how alone she had been all this time. I wanted to strangle her father. It was a shame I wouldn't get the chance. How the fuck had he done this to her?

My parents walked down the stairs and I waited. I wanted to say something to her, but I wasn't sure what. Explaining my "average" comment would sound insincere now.

"I'll bring him over when he's ready," she told me, then opened the door and stepped inside before I could say anything else.

"Come on, son. Let them alone," my father called after me.

Frustrated as hell, I turned and followed my parents home.

When we got to the house, my mother looked back at me. "I don't know what you think is attractive, but apparently Dustin was the only one with good taste in women. That girl is a beauty. Even just out of bed she is breathtaking. Nothing fake about her. She's the real thing. She'll make a man a good wife one day. Shame you can't see what a jewel she is." Then she turned and walked inside.

Dad chuckled and I looked over at him. "What?" I snapped.

He only laughed harder. "Reckon that 'average' comment was about the stupidest shit I've ever heard. I may be an old man, but I ain't blind. Hell, boy, she's a looker. She left average a long time ago. But then, you know that. Be careful what you say, because your momma will make sure the world knows."

He continued to laugh as he went inside.

I glanced back at her house and remembered the young girl who used to run across the street in bare feet and a pair of cutoff jeans and a shirt tied up above her belly button. All that red hair flying, and her smile big and bright. Dustin would meet her out front, and she'd fling herself into his arms and he would swing her around.

I think it was about the time she had turned sixteen that I decided staying away from her was really fucking important. Because I had watched her run into my brother's arms, and I'd been jealous. The emotion had startled me and taken me a moment to understand. I'd never been jealous before or after. Because I had known in that moment that I'd somehow lost a part of my soul to a girl who would never be mine.

I spent the next seven years proving just how much I didn't need love. I just needed pussy, and I could get it easy. I had fucked Sienna Roy out of my system with each redhead who wasn't her. With each girl I bedded, I'd felt further and further away from the pain.

When Sienna had left, she'd taken a piece of me with her.

I had suffered, and I was so trashed for months that I couldn't even remember half the shit I did. I had wanted her, and she had been my brother's. She had also been too damn young.

I was a fuckup and would never be good enough for the likes of her. My brother was what she'd deserved. Someone like him was *still* what she deserved. Not me. Never me. I wasn't good enough. I wasn't a golden boy. I couldn't make her happy. But I'd be damned if I let anything hurt her again. I could protect her. And Micah. They weren't mine, but in my heart they were.

Chapter Eight

SIENNA

"What if I told you that Dewayne was your daddy's older brother? Would you like having Dewayne as an uncle?"

Micah went very still in my arms, and his frown grew. This was not how I wanted to do this with him. I was hoping to watch *Star Wars* with him and have that as a happy distraction. But after our morning visitors I knew this had to be done now. I wanted him to have Tabby and Dave Falco in his life, and from what I had just seen, they did too. It was time Micah had grandparents to dote on him.

"Dewayne is my daddy's brother? But . . . he didn't tell me that."

This was the tricky part. Micah was five, but our life had made him grow up fast. Emotionally, he was a lot older than he should've had to be.

"Dewayne didn't know about you until the other day, when you thought he made me cry. I had thought he knew. I'd sent letters, but they never got them."

"Who's they?" Micah asked.

"Dewayne's parents. Your daddy's parents. Your grandparents."

Micah's eyes went wide with wonder. "Mama T and Dave are my grandparents?"

I nodded. "And they want to know you very much. They loved your daddy a whole bunch. And they want to know his son. That's why they came over this morning. They're very excited to know you're their grandson."

Micah's eyes got bigger. "I have grandparents? I thought you said I didn't."

Sighing, I kissed his head. "I didn't want you to think that your grandparents didn't love you. I thought they were turning their backs on us since your daddy was gone. So I was protecting you."

Micah was quiet for several minutes. I let him think about all this and didn't speak. He fiddled with his thumbs as he studied his hands. Every once in a while he glanced back over his shoulder, out the window to the house across the street. I couldn't imagine what was going on in his little head. Saving him from any more pain was my first concern.

"Do they have pictures of my daddy?" he asked. I'd only had a couple in my purse when I had been shipped off, and that was all Micah had seen of his father.

I nodded. "They have a lot. You will even see pictures of him when he was your age. You can see just how much you look like him."

Micah fidgeted and looked out the window toward their house. "Can I go see the pictures and have some cookies?" he asked, turning back to me.

Tabby would probably never be without chocolate chip cookies again. "I am sure they are waiting anxiously for you to go over there. Do you want me to come too? Or would you like me to let you visit alone?"

Sending him over there alone terrified me. I wanted to hold his hand through this, but just like through everything else, Micah was a rock. He handled things with a strength that was unexpected from a five-year-old.

"I want you there. She makes really good cookies. You can eat some too."

I wanted to let out a sigh of relief.

"Okay, then. Let me get dressed and brush my hair, and then we can walk over there. Why don't you go get dressed too?" He was still wearing his Superman pajamas.

He nodded and hopped up, then ran off. This had been much easier than I'd anticipated. But then, he hadn't had time for it to sink in yet.

I followed behind him and went to the bathroom. Before I did anything else, I stood there and looked at myself. I had always thought I was pretty. Guys seemed to like me. I wasn't a raving beauty or anything, but my body wasn't bad. My legs were long and I had C-cup boobs. My hair was red, but I had made my peace with that a long time ago, as well as the freckles on my nose. But knowing Dewayne had described me as average stung. No . . . it was a serious blow to my self-esteem. Maybe I had aged more than I realized. Maybe being a struggling single mom had put some wear and tear on me. I leaned toward the mirror and checked for wrinkles. I did see my freckles, but no wrinkles yet. I guess my nose was kind of stubby and my arms weren't that toned. I didn't have time for the gym. Any sign of a tan had faded.

I guess I was average. He hadn't called me ugly, at least. I could live with average. Besides, I was Micah's mom—who cared what a man thought of me? It wasn't like I was looking to start dating. If that were the case, I might have spent a little more time than usual making myself look less worn out.

When I was finished brushing my teeth and brushing my hair, I wanted to slap myself for letting Dewayne's opinion affect me. I was better than that. I was tougher than that. Being pretty wasn't something I worried about normally. I went to my closet, pulled out a pair of shorts, and pulled them on, then grabbed a tank top. I would not think about my clothing choices. I was not going to dress nicer than this for a visit across the street. I intended to do some yard work today and have a picnic in the backyard with my son. No reason to dress up. I'd already spent more time on my face than was necessary for those activities.

I slipped my feet into a pair of flip-flops and refused to care that I hadn't painted my toenails since taking off the old polish last week. It did not matter. At all.

"You ready, Momma?" Micah asked as he bounced on the balls of his feet, looking out the screen door toward the Falcos' house. He was anxious to see them again now that he knew they were his family.

"Yes, sir," I replied, reaching for his hand and opening the door. "Let's go meet your grandparents."

"I already met them, Momma. Remember?"

I nodded. "Yes, you did, but this time will be different because now they know how important you are to them."

Micah seemed to take that in as he started walking toward the street, pulling me with him. Dewayne's truck was still in the driveway, and although I knew he needed to see Micah and talk to him now that Micah knew he was family, I kind of wished he had left.

As much as I shouldn't care about the "average" comment, it had hurt my feelings, and it was going to make me feel uncomfortable around him. I hated that. I wished I could just get over it. That teenage crush I had on Dewayne was rearing its ugly head and taunting me with his opinion of me. Men sucked.

DEWAYNE

Momma stood at the door, watching Micah and Sienna walk toward the house. She was wringing her hands, barely able to contain herself. She'd been watching their house ever since we got back home. I was glad Sienna wasn't going to make her wait. She had talked to Micah right away, it looked like.

Figures the kid would be curious and want to come over. He was like his dad in that way.

"Look at him. He's so perfect. Looks just like Dustin," Momma breathed in awe as they walked up the front steps.

"Open the door for them, Momma," I told her.

Dad stood up from his spot on the sofa and walked over to join her as they greeted their grandson. Dad's hand settled on Momma's shoulder, and she reached back to squeeze his hand. This was good for them. Micah was gonna be good for them.

Momma opened the door just as Micah arrived. He studied her for a moment, then looked at Dad. Everyone remained silent, waiting on him to say something. Finally he shrugged and held out his arms. "So, I'm your grandson."

His statement caused everyone to relax, and both my parents started laughing. Then Momma bent down and held her arms out to him. "Yes, you are, and I'd really like a hug from my grandson."

Micah went into her arms willingly. His gaze met mine across the room, and he smiled. "Hey, Uncle Dewayne," he said.

Nothing in my life had prepared me for that. I managed not to make an idiot of myself by getting emotional like a fucking woman and nodded. "Hey, little man," I replied with a grin.

He pulled away from Momma and looked up at her seriously. "You got any cookies?" he asked.

Momma's laughter was musical and light. I hadn't heard that in a really long time. "Yes, I do. I made a batch just for you. Come on in the kitchen."

"First I need my hug," Dad said, and Micah walked over to him as Dad bent down to hug him.

"You're really big. My daddy was really big like my uncle Dewayne. I seen pictures. Do you have pictures of him?"

Dad tensed up for a moment, then relaxed. We hadn't looked at photos of Dustin since his death. We never even talked about him. But this kid was gonna want to talk about him.

"Yeah, we got lots of photos of your daddy. We can look at 'em together," he said, and Micah beamed up at him excitedly.

"You hear that, Momma? You were right! They got lots of pictures of Daddy," he said, looking back at Sienna.

It was the first time since they'd walked in the house that I'd allowed myself to actually look at her. And it was a mistake because, damn it all to hell, she had on shorts and a tight little shirt that showed just how above average she was. Her hair was brushed into silky waves, and I missed the mussed look from this morning. I wanted to muss it up again. While those legs were wrapped around me.

No! Fuck! I had to stop that shit. She was Micah's mom. Not a fuck buddy.

"Come on in, young lady. We have cookies for you, too," Dad told Sienna, who hadn't spoken yet.

She blushed and glanced at me, then back at my dad. "I'm okay. Probably shouldn't eat cookies this early in the morning."

Dad put his arm around her shoulders. "Cookies are for all hours of the day. Don't you know that? I remember when you ate Tabby's cookies whenever you stepped foot in that door."

"I was younger and in better shape then," she replied, her blush getting worse.

What the hell was she talking about? The woman had curves in all the right places. It didn't get better than that.

"You're still a spring chicken. Better eat those cookies now. Middle age will change all that. Eat 'em while you're young."

Sienna laughed and walked with my dad to the kitchen. I remained where I was, unsure where I fit in here. It was my parents' house, but suddenly I felt like the outsider.

"Uncle Dewayne! Come eat these cookies with me. Mama T has real milk, too," Micah called out to me.

Then again, maybe I did have a place.

Chapter Nine

SIENNA

The Falcos hadn't been ready to let Micah leave. He'd been catered to all day long, and he was eating up all the attention. Dewayne had left around four, telling Micah bye and that he'd see him soon.

Shortly after Dewayne left, I'd tried to leave with Micah because I still hadn't gone to the grocery store. I always went on Sundays to get ready for the week. Micah, however, had latched on to the idea of staying with Tabby and Dave while I did my grocery shopping. So I let him.

I wasn't sure if I could remember a time when I'd gone grocery shopping without Micah. He was always with me, so I was used to telling him no and talking him out of sugary snacks. This was a much quieter and rather peaceful experience. I loved my son, but I decided I liked grocery shopping without him.

I took my time walking down each aisle and thinking about what we needed and how much money I had to work with. I kept a calculator in my purse for shopping because I had tried doing the math in my head but it's embarrassing when you get to the checkout and have to take things out of bags and give them back because you don't have enough money.

With no rent, we had more than we normally did for food, and it was nice to be able to splurge on the mint chocolate chip ice cream that Micah loved and some lemon tea for me. I stopped in front of the bread and looked for a sandwich bread that was healthy but still looked white enough that I could trick Micah into eating it. I also had to find one that didn't cost too much. Five dollars for a loaf of bread was ridiculous. Most of the time I could find a honey wheat that was light enough that Micah wouldn't complain.

"Bread is a serious matter. I can tell you agree," a masculine voice said beside me, and I turned around to see a tall, dark-haired man who looked to be at least thirty. His slacks and button-down shirt might have been one reason he looked older, and the crinkles around his eyes when he smiled aged him. He wasn't bad-looking, though.

"Pleasing my picky son is the trick," I explained. Normally, if I brought up my son, the men backed off. If this one was going to attempt to flirt with me, I might as well go ahead and send him on his way.

The man nodded, still grinning. "Yeah, I understand that completely. My niece always goes for the white bread when she comes to visit. She's nine, and her mother won't buy it at home. I'm the rule-breaking uncle."

He picked out a loaf of the more expensive white bread and winked at me. "I have to break a few rules every once in a while to feel cool. My job makes me so uncool I need a little pick-me-up now and again."

He was better than okay. He was actually really cute. He had that clean-cut look that I wasn't a big fan of, but he wore it well.

"Really? What uncool job is it that you have?" I asked, surprising myself. I normally didn't encourage conversations with men. But I liked this one. He was friendly, and it didn't feel like he was trying to pick me up in the bread aisle.

"Vice principal at Sea Breeze High," he replied, then let out a sigh and shook his head. "Major letdown, I know."

A vice principal. He was young to be a vice principal. Or maybe he was older than I'd first assumed.

"That can't be an easy job," I replied, finally reaching for a bread I thought would work.

"It's not so bad. But then there are days like today when I've been dealing with work while I'm supposed to be enjoying my weekend, then bump into a beautiful woman studying bread."

Beautiful woman. He had no idea how nice that was to hear. It was a balm to my ego, which Dewayne had squished rather flat this morning. He wasn't as devastatingly gorgeous as Dewayne, nor could he be considered sexy exactly. But he was attractive, and he had a kind smile. He was definitely more in my league.

"Was that too strong? Should I have been smoother?" the guy asked, and I had to laugh.

I shook my head. "No. I was just thinking about how nice it was to be called beautiful," I explained.

He frowned. "I would assume you get that a lot."

Not really. The guys who normally hit on me called me hot or just flat asked me out. Then there were the guys who thought I was average. *Ugh!* I had to let that go.

I smiled and held out my hand to shake his. "Sienna Roy," I said, deciding I liked the guy enough to exchange names.

He slipped his larger hand in mine and shook it. "Nice to meet you, Sienna. Cam Dodge."

He didn't let my hand go right away, but firmly held it a second longer than necessary.

"So, Sienna, what is it you do? Other than shop for bread for your son?"

"I'm a hairdresser," I replied.

"And I'm assuming you're not married. I did the whole casual glance-at-the-ring-finger thing when I walked up and got a good look at you."

Laughing, I shook my head. "No. Not married."

He nodded, and the easygoing smile on his face became

more hopeful. "Let's say I asked you to dinner Friday night. . . . Would you go?"

He was sweet. The cockiness that I was used to in guys was missing, and I liked that a lot. I normally said no to dates because of Micah, but now that the Falcos were in his life, they'd probably love the opportunity to keep him on Friday night. Sure, my body and maybe my heart wanted Dewayne, but it wasn't like there was a chance of that ever happening. Crap! I had to stop thinking about Dewayne. He was Micah's uncle, that was it. Letting him sneak into my thoughts like this would just end up causing me heartache.

"I need to discuss it with my son. Make sure he's good with me going out. We normally do popcorn and a movie." I was telling this man way more than was normal for me. . . .

Cam grinned and held out his phone. "Why don't you put your number in here for me, and then I'll text you so you'll have my number. You can call me when you've spoken to your son."

He wasn't spooked by the idea of Micah at all. This was a first.

I took his phone and punched in my number, then handed it back to him. "Here you go," I said after texting myself. "I've already sent a message to my phone. I'll let you know about Friday no later than tomorrow."

He gave me a crooked grin that was really very cute, then nodded toward the next aisle. "Guess I better go get some peanut butter to go with this bread. I'll be looking forward to hearing from you, Sienna Roy," he said, then turned and walked away.

I actually might have a date, I thought. *A real date.*

DEWAYNE

Micah had visited my parents' house two afternoons this week, Monday and Tuesday. Momma had called to tell me everything he said and everything he did while he was there. She was fascinated by the kid. I was pretty damn thankful for him myself. I hadn't seen my mother this happy in a long time.

Momma had called me this morning to let me know that she had to take Dad in for his routine exam at his cardiologist and wouldn't be home this afternoon. She was worried about Micah not getting to come visit. I had assured her he would understand, but she hadn't seemed too convinced. So I'd told her I would take dinner over to Sienna's and eat with them. That had pacified her.

I was eventually going to have to talk to Momma about this. She'd smother Sienna if she kept this up. Sienna had been great about letting Micah go visit for a couple of hours every afternoon, but I was expecting her to limit this soon. It had been just her and Micah for five years. She wasn't going to let my momma take her boy away all the time. I expected Momma to convince her to let Micah start coming to her house after school. It would help Sienna save money and I was sure she'd like the idea of him not having to go to after-school care. I just didn't know if Sienna was ready for that yet.

Pulling my truck into Sienna's driveway, I winced at the sight of her beat-up car. I didn't like Micah riding around in that piece of shit. It was dangerous. Sienna's pride would be a hurdle. It was the only reason I hadn't brought her a new car already. I knew she wouldn't accept it. I had to find a way to make her accept it.

The front door swung open, and Micah came running out onto the porch, waving at me with a big grin.

When I had called Sienna and asked her if I could bring dinner and visit with Micah, she had seemed reluctant at first. She was keeping her distance from me, and I understood that. I was okay with it. Hell, I needed it. Getting close to her would be a huge mistake. I was going to take care of her and the kid, but I wasn't going to get too close to her in the process.

I reached over and grabbed the two large pizzas in my passenger seat. Micah would be coming after me if I didn't hurry, and I didn't want him to see the six-pack on the floor. I stepped out of the truck and made my way to the porch.

"You brought pizza! I love pizza! I love mac 'n' cheese better, but I love real pizza. It's better than the bread kind," Micah said, grinning. Then his smile fell, and he glanced back at the house with a concerned frown.

I started to ask him what was wrong, when he swung his big eyes back to me. He looked upset. "Don't tell Momma I said that 'bout the bread pizzas. It'll hurt her feelings. She makes 'em 'cause they're cheap."

The boy was protecting his momma again. Made my chest fill with pride and an ache at the same time. He was just a baby, but he acted like the man of the house. He shouldn't have that kind of responsibility on his little shoulders.

"It'll be our secret," I assured him, lowering my voice.

He looked relieved, and a smile replaced his frown. "Momma said you were getting me one with lots of cheese," he said, excited again.

I realized that pizza like this was a luxury for these two. Which pissed me off all over again. Why the hell had Sienna's parents done this to her and Micah? Sienna and Micah shouldn't have had to suffer so much. My parents would have made sure they had everything they needed, and a fucking pizzeria pizza wouldn't be a treat.

"Momma made some sweet tea, and Mama T brought over a whole basket of cookies this morning. But Momma said we gotta wait until dessert to eat 'em."

I started to respond, but then Sienna filled the doorway and my tongue suddenly stuck to the roof of my mouth. She was dressed in a pair of cutoff jean shorts and a fitted George Strait T-shirt from a tour nine years ago. She had been only thirteen then, and I knew the Roys hadn't let her go to the George Strait concert at the Wharf that year.

"Nice shirt," I said, needing an excuse for looking at her curves. Perfectly delicious curves. Ones I wanted to run my hands over and brand with a trail of bites. Marking my path . . . *Stop!* No. I couldn't do that.

"Dustin got it for me. I used it as a sleep shirt for years because it was too big. He went with friends, and you took them, I believe," she said with a small smile.

I had taken them, but I'd forgotten. Dustin hadn't wised up yet and made sure everyone knew Sienna was his, and she was changing back then. Guys were noticing her. He'd bought her a shirt, though, when I'd pointed out to him that she'd probably hear he had taken Victoria Harris to the concert. Victoria hadn't been as pretty as Sienna back then, and she wasn't anywhere near the looker Sienna was now. My brother had been obsessed with Victoria's tits. That had been it.

So he had bought that T-shirt for Sienna. Funny how that was a memory I had pushed away. But seeing Sienna in that shirt brought it all back.

"I remember taking them. It wasn't a great concert. You didn't miss much," I told her.

She laughed, and everything around her lit up. The sound of her laughter made all that was wrong seem right. "I know that's a lie. But thanks for trying. Victoria Harris made sure I knew just how amazing that concert had been. She also made sure I knew that although I got the T-shirt, she got the guy." Sienna smirked. "That was all before, though."

Before. Before I forced my brother to wake the hell up and see what was right there for him to take. Sienna had worshipped him and he had loved it, but he hadn't been ready to do anything remotely exclusive. Until I had lunch with her and until she caught the attention of every male at Sea Breeze High. That had lit a fire under Dustin's ass.

"Come on in with those pizzas. I've already got the table set." She stepped back so I could walk inside.

"Do I need to fill the cups with ice?" Micah asked her.

"That would be very helpful," she told him.

He hurried off around me and into the kitchen. I set the pizzas down in the center of the table while he tugged a chair over to get cups down. I moved to go help him but Sienna's hand touched my arm.

"Don't help him. Let him do it," she said in a whisper.

This was why he was so responsible for his age. Sienna let him feel important. I wasn't sure if I liked the idea of him not getting a chance to be a kid or if this was good training. Maybe she was raising a better man than me or my brother had been. God knows I loved my momma, but she waited on my brother and me hand and foot. Can't say it helped either of us much.

Chapter Ten

SIENNA

I silently ate my one slice of pizza while listening to Micah tell Dewayne everything Dewayne could possibly want to know and then some. I enjoyed savoring the pizza. It was delicious, and I was being careful to take small bites. There was no way I could eat two slices in front of Dewayne. I didn't normally care how much I ate in front of men. But knowing that Dewayne would be thinking how much I didn't need a second slice would make it hard to eat.

Besides, Dewayne had eaten five slices, and Micah was on his second slice. They were doing a fine job of putting the pizzas away themselves. Watching Micah enjoy the cheesy pizza was worth sitting through this with Dewayne.

When Dewayne had asked if he could bring dinner and visit Micah tonight, I had wanted to make up an excuse. I wanted to relax after work, and being near Dewayne was not relaxing. But I knew how much Micah would love this, so I had said okay. And now here I sat, taking the world's smallest bites of a slice of pizza while my stomach growled from missing lunch today. When Dewayne left, I was going to eat a piece of leftover pizza. Maybe two.

"Isn't that right, Momma?" Micah said, and I snapped back to attention and blinked, focusing on my son.

"Uh, is what right?" I asked, feeling like an idiot.

"Don't you have a date tomorrow night?"

What? Why was he talking about that? I had asked him if he cared, and then I'd talked to Tabby, who had been thrilled that I was going on a date with Vice Principal Dodge. However, this wasn't Dewayne's business.

I simply nodded and shoved a larger bite of pizza in my mouth.

"He's a principal," Micah added with pride. He had taken the idea of me dating much better than I'd anticipated.

"Principal?" Dewayne asked, his eyes now completely focused on me.

I swallowed the pizza and took a drink of water. Then I nodded and forced a smile. "Vice principal."

"Seriously?" Dewayne asked, not looking happy about this at all. "I thought you said you didn't date. You had Micah and that was enough."

Whoa . . . wait a minute. Anger simmered in my blood, and

I sat up straighter and leaned forward, glaring at Dewayne with a warning I hoped he understood. "If I get asked out by a nice man who doesn't think I'm average, that's my decision. I did ask Micah how he felt first, and then I spoke with Tabby before agreeing to this date. His name is Cam Dodge and he's the vice principal at the high school. Your mother was thrilled."

Dewayne clenched his jaw and didn't flinch. "Where did you meet Cam Dodge?"

I was done. This was over. I stood up and threw my napkin on the table. "None of your business," I informed him, and began clearing off the table.

"She met him in the bread aisle at the grocery store. He was really nice to her," Micah offered since I wasn't talking. That kid didn't know when to keep information to himself.

"The bread aisle?" Dewayne asked, as if he was horrified by the idea.

After setting dirty dishes in the sink, I took several deep breaths before turning around to face him again. He was welcome into Micah's life, but he was not welcome into mine. I didn't need his approval.

Just looking at him made me crack just a little. I hated that he affected me like that. I placed my hands on my hips. "Yes, Dewayne, the bread aisle. We discussed white bread and its healthy alternatives. He was nice to me. It felt good. Six years, Dewayne. Six very long years. I think I'm due a dinner date."

Dewayne flinched this time. I smiled at him, although it didn't reach my eyes. I was angry. I wanted him to leave. But he was here for Micah. It was time I gave them some alone time.

"I'm going to soak in the bath while you two play. Come get me when Dewayne leaves," I told Micah. Then I forced my gaze back to Dewayne. "Thanks for dinner. It was delicious."

I turned and walked toward the hallway.

"You barely ate any of it," Dewayne called out to me.

"Don't want to gain any weight and dip below that average line I'm walking," I replied, then slammed my bedroom door behind me.

Squeezing my eyes closed, I took several calming breaths, then began to strip. I was ready for a long soak in the tub with the new bath salts Hillary had given me to try out. She wanted her employees to sample products she carried at the salon so we could recommend them. I loved that idea because I would never let myself splurge on things like bath salts.

Micah's laughter in the living room reminded me why Dewayne was here, and I let my anger and frustration with him go. He had come to see Micah. He was protecting Micah. As insulting as it was for him to question my choices, I was glad he wanted to be a part of Micah's life. I needed to learn to take the bad with the good.

From now on when Dewayne came to visit Micah, I would just take really long baths. I could eat more in here too. It was a win-win situation. The good thing about Dewayne being a jerk was that at least I wasn't going all silly around him. His beautiful body and face didn't get to me anymore.

Well, almost.

"Momma, I'm taking Dewayne outside to show him Daddy's star. Okay?" Micah called through the door a long time later.

I had gone outside with him last night to help him find the biggest star we could see. He believed it was Dustin. So I let him believe it.

DEWAYNE

When Sienna had called out good-bye to me last night through her closed bedroom door, I knew I'd really screwed up. For starters, I was going to have to explain the "average" comment to her, because it was bothering her. She kept bringing it up.

Then I needed to remember that she had done a damn fine job of raising Micah on her own. Trusting her was important. I did trust her. It was this Cam Dodge I didn't trust. I was going to fix that, too. I would talk to him. See what I thought about him. If he was a good guy, then I'd encourage this dating thing with Sienna. If he wasn't, I'd make sure he stayed the hell away from her.

Last night when Micah took me outside to see the star he believed was Dustin, I should have had a moment with him. It should have been the only thing on my mind. But it wasn't. I'd been planning this visit to Cam Dodge. Fucker messed up my night. I had to make sure he was worth it. Sienna deserved the best.

Pulling my truck into the visitor parking at the high school, I decided this was the best idea. The man couldn't ignore me if I showed up at his job. I'd ask for a meeting with him and then we'd talk. Sienna wouldn't know about it, and I could hopefully step back and let her date.

Maybe she'd smile at me again. And fucking eat something around me.

I stepped into the school office, and Mrs. Quinn looked up at me. She broke into a smile as she stood up. The short little secretary was older than my momma, and her white hair was always curled up tight, her bangs pinned back with a bow like she was seven instead of seventy. Couldn't help but love the woman.

"Well, if it ain't Dewayne Falco come to pay us a visit. I've heard that you cause less trouble these days now that your buddies have all been tamed by their women."

Leave it to Mrs. Quinn to know about everyone's lives. She may be stuck sitting behind that desk and dealing with teenagers all day five days a week, but when we graduated, she didn't forget us. People like her were who we needed in education.

"I came to see that pretty smile of yours," I told her, then winked just to watch her blush and bat her eyelashes.

"Still a charmer, I see," she replied, beaming at me. I was

sure she didn't get flirted with often, given that she was as wide as she was tall. Still, she deserved some attention.

"Yes, ma'am. I always think a pretty woman needs to be told just that."

She waved me off and giggled, which was hilarious coming from someone her age. When she retired, it would be a sad day for Sea Breeze High.

"I know you didn't just come here to flirt with me. Now, what can we do for you, Mr. Falco?" she asked, still smiling.

I nodded at the door I knew belonged to the vice principal. Back when I was in school, the vice principal had been Old Man Warldo. He was grumpy and mean as hell. It was good news for kids in Sea Breeze when the man retired two years ago.

"I need to see Mr. Dodge," I told her, trying to be as respectful as possible. If I could get through Mrs. Quinn, then I was home free.

She looked unsure, then picked up her phone and pressed a button.

"Mr. Dodge, are you available to meet with Mr. Dewayne Falco, sir?"

The man wasn't going to know who the hell I was. "Tell him it's concerning Sienna Roy," I told her. That would pique his interest.

Mrs. Quinn's eyes went big, and I knew she recognized that name too. My brother's death had been a tragedy this whole school had suffered. And Sienna's leaving had shocked everyone.

"Uh, it's concerning Miss Sienna Roy," she added, studying me while she said it. "Yes, sir. I'll send him right in."

He was curious. Good.

She hung up and raised her eyebrows. "Is Sienna Roy back home?"

I nodded. "Yeah, she is."

Mrs. Quinn let out what looked like a sigh of relief. "Well, glory be. It's about time. That sweet girl was shipped off, and I knew it wasn't right. Worried me sick. Glad she's been able to come home. Reckon her father's passing made that possible."

How this woman knew so much, I didn't know. But she did. She seemed to know a lot. I just nodded.

She waved her hand toward Cam Dodge's door. "Go on in. Mr. Dodge said he would see you."

I thanked her and headed for the door before he could change his mind.

Cam Dodge stood up from behind his desk when I opened the door. He was young. I was expecting someone older, and that had bothered me. But he was young, and fuck it all if that didn't bother me more.

His button-down shirt and pressed slacks were part of the uniform, but he looked like he was comfortable in that fancy shit. He was smiling, but his smile was very unsure. The name

Sienna Roy had been the reason he'd agreed to see me. So now he wanted to know why I wanted to see him. Well, he'd have to wait. I had some things I wanted to know first.

"How old are you?" I asked, not sitting down but standing on the other side of the desk, crossing my arms over my chest and meeting his curious gaze. I liked that I had to look down at him. He was a good two or three inches shorter than me.

"Excuse me?" he said, his forehead wrinkling.

"I asked how old you were," I repeated. If he wanted more information from me, he'd need to answer that first.

"Twenty-eight," he replied, still watching me with an unsure expression.

"You normally pick women up at the grocery store?" I asked.

His eyebrows shot up in surprise. "No," he replied. "Who are you, exactly?" he asked, clearly being careful.

"Mrs. Quinn told you who I was. You ever been married?"

His eyes went wide with surprise, then he narrowed them in agitation. "I don't see how that is your business, seeing as I don't know who you are. I was told your name, but all I know is you are someone connected to the woman I have a date with tonight. I'd like more information from you if you intend to grill me."

He spoke like a principal. I watched him fiddle with his tie and stick his hands in his pockets while he stood tall. The dude was a nerd. He wasn't anywhere near Sienna's league. What was she doing with this guy?

"Sienna's son is my nephew. Since she met you in the bread aisle of a grocery store, I'd like to know more about you before you take her out tonight. I'm also going to make sure you understand that her safety is really fucking important. You hurt her, and you won't live long enough to regret it."

The man flinched. At least he believed me. He took in my tattooed arms and the piercing in my lip before meeting my gaze again. He cleared his throat. "You're her son's uncle . . . but you aren't her brother? Does that mean you're the boy's father's brother?" he asked.

I nodded.

He studied me a moment. "Is the boy's father still in her life?"

I shook my head. "You don't get to ask questions. You asked her out. I'm asking the questions. Have you been married? I'm assuming you don't have a record, since you're a principal. The school board would have checked that shit. But do you have a girlfriend? Or a drinking problem? Drugs?"

Cam held up his hands and laughed nervously. "Whoa. Okay. Wow. No to all of that. I'm completely clean and unattached. I was engaged five years ago, but she had cervical cancer, and she didn't make it."

His slight wince when he mentioned his fiancée's death didn't go unnoticed. He was a man trying to move on. He had a good job, and he seemed pretty damn sincere. This was not enough for me, but I'd ask around and find out more about him. My gut was telling me he was safe.

"Don't hurt her," I repeated. "That means touching her in ways she doesn't want, or touching at all. Remember, I'll know and I'll come after you. I've got a fucking record, and I'm not scared of prison."

I turned and walked out of the small office, and waved good-bye to Mrs. Quinn before leaving.

I had some more poking around to do about the guy, and only eight hours left to do it.

Chapter Eleven

SIENNA

I wasn't ready to introduce Cam to Micah. I wasn't sure if I would ever go out with Cam again after tonight. There was always a chance it wouldn't go well. I hardly knew this man. No reason to introduce him to the most important person in my life. That would be for later, if I liked him and wanted to spend more time with him. Tabby agreed, and she'd had Micah come over an hour before Cam was supposed to show up.

It also gave me time to change clothes five times and fuss with my hair. Micah would have been right under me, asking me why I was changing clothes so much and messing with my hair. He would then tell Dewayne, which would be humiliating. I already knew he didn't think there was much that could be done with me.

Fortunately, Cam disagreed with him. That eased my mind some, and I put back on the skirt I had tried on first and slipped on my wraparound blouse. This was casual but nice. It would work for anywhere. I slipped on a pair of black pumps and fought the urge to go pull my hair back up again. Letting it hang loose had been my last-minute decision, but now I was questioning it.

The doorbell stopped me from doing anything more. I gave myself a quick pep talk in the mirror and then headed for the door. It had been a very long time since I'd been on a date. I didn't know how to do this, especially with someone I didn't know. I'd only ever dated one guy, and Dustin had been my best friend. I'd known everything about him.

"You can do this," I said one last time before opening the door.

Cam was dressed in a pair of khaki pants and a light blue polo shirt. I had dressed appropriately. One worry off my list.

"Hello," he said with a grin. "You look gorgeous. I feel like I need to go back home and try to make myself look like it's actually believable that we're out together."

Yes, he was doing wonders for my self-esteem. "Thank you, but you look very handsome yourself. I don't think anyone will question that we are together."

He chuckled, then shrugged. "I'm not sure how you're that blind, but I'm just counting my lucky stars." He held out his arm to me. "Ready?"

I nodded and stepped outside onto the porch, then locked

up behind me before sticking my keys in my purse. I'd had a key made for Tabby this week and given it to her, so if she needed to get inside to get Micah anything, she'd be able to.

"I made reservations at Le Cellier. I hope you like steak," he said with a smile. I had heard of Le Cellier, but I'd never been there.

"I love steak," I told him. And I intended to eat a filet, which felt nice. I wouldn't have to pick at my food because I was worrying about what he was thinking. This was going to be a good night. I could already tell.

Two hours later I was ready to go back home and put on my pajamas. Cam was really nice, but I was a little bored with him. He talked about work and asked me about myself. He did everything right, but there was something missing. I wasn't sure if I was just being picky because my last relationship had been with someone I was already so close to.

"You want to stop in Live Bay and listen to Jackdown play? I hear they're good. I haven't been to see Jackdown yet, but Live Bay seems to be the place to go to hear live music and dance."

For the first time all night, something sounded exciting. I hadn't been dancing in forever . . . since the prom, and I wasn't sure that counted. I danced with Micah all the time around the house, but live music and actual dancing sounded like fun. Maybe it had been the stuffy fancy restaurant he had taken me to that had bored me. If he liked to dance, he couldn't be completely boring.

"Sounds like fun," I said, trying not to bounce in my seat like a kid.

He pulled his Volvo into the parking lot. The place was packed. I soaked it all in. This was a world I didn't know. One I wanted a taste of. Live Bay had been around when I was sixteen, but I hadn't been old enough to get inside. Now I was getting to see what the fuss was all about.

"Isn't that your . . . uh, son's uncle?" Cam asked.

I swung my gaze over to where he was looking and immediately wished I hadn't. Seeing Dewayne pressing some girl up against his truck while attacking her face was not what I wanted to see. I was sure she was gorgeous. Surprisingly enough, she had red hair. That's all I could see of her. Maybe my hair needed to be a lighter red for Dewayne. She also looked tan. I didn't have time to get tanned. I should make time. I could play outside with Micah and get a tan.

Wait . . . How did Cam know who Dewayne was?

I tore my gaze off Dewayne and the lucky female to look at Cam. "How do you know Dewayne?" I asked. Had he researched me? If he had, I wasn't sure how I felt about that. It seemed creepy.

Cam pressed his lips together as if he was thinking hard about something. Crap. I needed to get away from this man. He could have stalked me! "Dewayne paid me a visit at work today.

He wanted to check me out before you went out with me."

I didn't have any words. None at all. I didn't have to ask Dewayne to know that Cam was telling the truth. It was something Dewayne would do. He didn't trust me to keep Micah safe, so he was doing that for me. I understood that to an extent, but he had crossed the line. I wasn't going to let him walk into my private life and stick his nose where it didn't belong. Maybe I should find out who that woman was who currently had her tongue down his throat. If he was going to be around Micah, I deserved to know if she was suitable.

"Stop the car," I ordered, and Cam didn't argue. He put the car in park, and I jumped out without an explanation and marched over to Dewayne, letting my anger burn brighter with each step. I hadn't thought this through, but in the moment I was so mad I didn't care.

I slapped him hard on the back without thinking that he could knock me across the parking lot with one swing. Luckily, I'd had the forethought to take a step away as Dewayne spun around and reached out to grab my arm. His eyes were bloodshot, and he was pissed. His grip on my arm made my knees buckle because it seriously felt like he was about to snap my arm in two. But I fought back a cry of pain and tried to keep the angry glare on my face.

The moment his eyes focused on me, he dropped my arm like it was on fire. "Fuck! Sienna, what the hell are you doing?"

I would not cradle my abused arm in front of him and the

bimbo behind him. Yes, I called her a bimbo, because now that I could see her, she looked like one. Seriously way too much makeup, and her breasts were bare.

"You," I said, pointing at Dewayne with the hand that was attached to my good arm. "You went to Cam's office today! How dare you question my decisions? When you're out here with"—I glanced at the woman who had thankfully pulled her shirt up over her chest—"her."

The girl frowned at me. "Who is this?" she asked in a pouty voice, and I realized her lips were pumped full of collagen. Ugh.

"I was protecting you. Someone needs to. You agreed to a date with a stranger at the grocery store, Sienna. I was making sure he wasn't a psycho."

"You had no right! I'm not bringing him around Micah. Not until I know him. So that means he is none of your business."

Dewayne raised his eyebrows and took a step toward me. His expression darkened. "Yeah, it is. I want Micah's momma safe."

Well, crap. I would not melt because he was being a protective, possessive bear. Just because I hadn't known what it felt like didn't mean I had to like it. Dang it.

"What about her? You're in Micah's life. Is *she* safe?" I asked.

Dewayne didn't even glance back at her or explain. He had been about to screw her right here in front of everyone, but now he was ignoring her. "I don't even know her name, Sienna. This is just fun, baby. I'll never see her again."

"Excuse me," the girl said, now more than annoyed.

My heart had decided to do a little flippy thing from him calling me baby. Which was ridiculous. He thought I was average, and now I knew why. I didn't wear enough makeup or show enough skin for him.

"It's what I do, Sienna. I don't do relationships or dates. You were going on a date with the guy. I had to make sure that he was a good man."

Okay. I didn't understand this world at all. Dewayne was still a man whore, apparently. I had never seen him in a relationship with a woman. Which was a shame because the territorial thing he did and the way he called me Little Red was pretty amazing. Even in his barbarian way he made me feel special. He was good at that.

Cam cleared his throat behind me, and I realized I had forgotten him in the car. I turned to him and gave him an apologetic smile. "Cam, you know Dewayne," I said, then glanced at Dewayne. "So, did he pass inspection?"

Dewayne didn't move his eyes off me. He held my gaze for a moment too long. The woman with him said something, but I was completely lost in his eyes. I had always loved his eyes. "Yeah, Little Red, he's safe."

I had forgotten how much I liked it. But that wasn't what struck me the most. It was the way he said "safe." As if he'd been let down by me. Hadn't he wanted me with someone safe?

"Take care of her," he said to Cam, then turned around

and took the girl's arm, and they walked back to the club.

Cam touched my sore arm, and I jerked. Crap, I had forgotten about that. It was still throbbing. "It's dark out here, but this looks like it's gonna be a helluva bruise. Let's get you home and get some ice on it. Unless you can't move it and you need me to take you to the hospital."

I made myself move it, and I could easily enough. I just winced and teared up.

"I'm good. I just need some ice," I assured him.

We didn't talk much on the way back to my house, and I figured this would be the last time Cam wanted to see me. Not that I could blame him.

The knocking on the front door broke me out of my thoughts as I stirred the sugar in my coffee. I walked to the door, wondering if Micah had already woken up and wanted to come home. I wanted to see him. When Tabby had told me he'd fallen asleep and asked if he could sleep over, I hadn't wanted to say yes. I had never been apart from Micah at night.

But the way Tabby's eyes lit up with hope made me give in, and I went home alone. Without Micah sleeping in his room beside mine, I hadn't slept well. I missed him. I wasn't sure how he would feel about waking up without me.

I opened the door to find Dewayne instead. Not who I wanted to see this morning. Not at all.

"We need to talk," he said, stepping inside like he owned the place. He may own a lot of things, but this house was mine.

I left the door open because I didn't like the idea of being closed up inside with him. I was mad at him. My arm had a black-and-blue bruise on it in the shape of his massive hand. I had taken ibuprofen last night and kept my arm on ice. Didn't seem to help. It hurt and it looked awful.

"Last night—" he said, then stopped as his eyes zeroed in on my bruised arm. I watched as he went pale, and I wasn't sure if he was going to pass out. It was ugly, but it wasn't that ugly.

"*Holy fuck,*" he swore, walking over to me and taking my wrist gently in his hand so he could lift my tender arm and look at it. "I did this?" he asked.

I just nodded. Who else did he think had grabbed me like he wanted to break me last night?

"I need to be shot," he said as he gently touched his fingertip to the marred skin. It was like a feather and, instead of hurting, caused me to shiver. "I didn't mean to hurt you. I'd never hurt you. Know that. I would *never hurt you.* I didn't know it was you last night when you slapped me, and I had drunk too damn much. My mind was slow, and it took me too long to register that it was you. God, Sienna, I'm so sorry."

His voice sounded so pained that I had to fight the urge to comfort him. Maybe slapping a man his size with his temper from behind had been a bad idea. . . .

"It's okay," I told him, then tugged my hand free of his and put some space between us.

"No, it's not. That isn't okay," he said, and his hands fisted up. "That will never happen again. I swear it. I'll fucking stop drinking. That shit is not okay. Ever."

Micah would be here soon, and after seeing Dewayne's reaction to my arm, I needed to change into something with longer sleeves. Micah would be upset too. I didn't want him scared of his uncle.

"Why are you here?" I asked, wanting him to get to the point before my son showed up.

"I came to talk about last night. To explain why I went to check out your date. But, shit, I can't get past your arm. I was worried about Cam, and I was the one who fucking hurt you. Did he know I did that?"

I nodded.

Dewayne's face darkened. "Fucker should have hit me. You need a man with some balls, and that dipshit knew I hurt you and didn't even come after me."

Was he kidding? Did he think everything should be handled with violence? And why was that so incredibly hot? I needed to seek mental help. Violence was not sexy. Even if Dewayne's muscles flexed when he was just talking about a fight.

"You need to leave," I told him before I could say something stupid.

Dewayne started to argue, but I held up my hand to stop him. "I know you didn't hurt me on purpose. I know you checked out Cam because you were protecting Micah and me. I get it. Now please leave. I need coffee, and I didn't sleep well last night, and I—"

I stopped talking as Dewayne took two steps toward me until he was towering over me. Then his larger-than-life hands cupped my face, and before anything could register, his lips were on mine.

I reached up and grabbed his arms to keep myself from melting into a puddle on the floor. Dewayne Falco's mouth was very talented, and the second his tongue slipped along my bottom lip, I opened up for him and was lost. The minty taste of him consumed me as he nibbled and explored my mouth. I just held on. It was all I could do. My entire body was under his command. I couldn't think coherently. Nothing had ever been like this. Ever.

But then, I had kissed only one other. And we had been just kids then.

Dewayne's hands slipped down my back and cupped my bottom as he lifted me higher up against his body. His tongue danced along and teased mine, driving me crazy.

A moan came from somewhere, but I wasn't sure whose it was. He heard it too, and it was like ice water over the fire that he'd wrapped us inside. Before I could steady myself, I was back on the ground and Dewayne was putting the length of my living room between us. I grabbed the chair behind me and hoped I didn't sway on my feet.

Dewayne's eyes were wild as he breathed heavily. At least he seemed as affected as I was. Because I was affected. No, I was marked. For life. I may not have been kissed by anyone other than Dustin before this, but I knew that no one was ever going to compare to what I'd just experienced.

"We can't. I shouldn't have," Dewayne said, shaking his head. Then he all but ran out of my house. I stood there and listened to his truck door close and the engine start up. I still stood there long after his truck had pulled out of my driveway.

He hadn't been able to get away from me fast enough. It wasn't like I had asked him to kiss me. Had he expected me to push him away? Was I a bad kisser? Had that moan been mine, and he had been turned off?

God! I hated being so damn clueless at this.

"Momma? Why is the door open?" Micah's voice asked, and I snapped out of my daze and turned to see my little boy frowning at me.

"Because I was waiting on you," I replied, not missing a beat.

He smiled and ran over to me, and I was careful to hide my bruised arm as I hugged him.

"Did you have fun?" I asked.

He nodded but pulled back and looked up at me. "I missed

you this morning. Mama T offered to make me biscuits, but I wanted to come home and eat Pop-Tarts with you. I remembered you didn't have work today."

Hillary had given me one Saturday off a month, and I was very thankful for that this morning. After what had just happened, leaving Dewayne at my house to watch Micah would have been hard and distracting.

"I can do better than Pop-Tarts. How about pancakes?" I asked him.

He grinned. "How about chocolate chip pancakes?"

"Sounds perfect," I said. "Let me go change shirts and we will get to work."

I didn't let him see me long enough to see my arm before I slipped out of the kitchen and into my bedroom, where I put on a long-sleeve T-shirt.

DEWAYNE

She was Dustin's. She would always be Dustin's.

Why the fuck had I kissed her? Goddamn, I wasn't going to be able to forget that. She'd been so damn sweet and hot all at once. Almost like she was innocent, when I knew she wasn't. She had a kid. She wasn't innocent, and she'd melted into my arms so easily. I had wanted to get her as close to me as fucking possible.

Then she'd moaned, and my dick had gone so hard it had

almost broken the damn zipper on my jeans. Fuck, but she was a sexy moaner. If I hadn't gotten away from her, I would have ended up fucking her on the sofa. The image of Sienna naked and wrapped around me sprang to mind, and I hit the steering wheel and cursed. I needed a fucking cigarette. Why did that shit have to kill you? Giving up alcohol was going to be a hell of a lot easier.

I couldn't do this shit. She was Micah's mom. She wasn't someone I could fuck for fun and walk away from, especially after today. Hell, not tasting her mouth again was going to kill me. No wonder my brother had knocked her up. Fuck! I wouldn't have been able to keep my wits about me when I was between her legs either. Damn woman could make any man lose his mind.

Dustin would want Sienna happy and taken care of. He would want her to have the life she deserved. Not one with his loser older brother, who had made more fucking mistakes than the average person. Hell, I'd bruised her arm. How the fuck did someone hurt Sienna? I wasn't drinking ever again. I was done. If that was the kind of shit I did when I was drunk, I wasn't touching alcohol. Sienna and Micah were going to turn me into the damn Pope.

Micah deserved a man in his life he could look up to. I would be the uncle who doted on him and made him feel loved, but I wasn't really much to look up to. I wasn't that guy. I never was and never would be good enough for Sienna Roy and my nephew. She needed a man who could be with just her. Who didn't need easy, no-strings fucks. And Micah needed a stable uncle. One who was a good role model. One who didn't fucking hurt his momma. *Motherfucker!* I wanted to beat my own ass. Sienna's bruised arm turned my stomach. I'd done that to her. I was the worthless piece of shit I knew wasn't worthy enough to kiss those sweet lips of hers.

Then I'd kissed her. What the hell! What kind of message did that send? Not a good one. Surely she knew I wasn't for her. I wasn't for anyone. I would have to talk to Sienna and apologize. She needed to understand that I couldn't be what she needed. I would be there for them, I would be her friend, I would take care of them—but that was all I was good for. Nothing more.

A knock on my window startled me, and I turned to see Marcus Hardy staring at me. I had parked in the lot of my apartment building, but I hadn't gotten out. I opened the door and stepped out of the truck.

"What was that about?" Marcus asked.

"What?" I asked, trying to blow off whatever it was he'd seen.

Marcus cocked an eyebrow at me. "Oh, I don't know. Maybe the snarling and cursing and hitting your steering wheel."

Shit. He'd been there awhile.

"Nothing," I replied, and started walking to my apartment. I knew Marcus would follow me.

"Preston said Sienna Roy was back and she has a kid."

Shit. Preston gossiped like a damn woman.

I nodded and pulled out my keys to unlock my apartment door.

"Kid's Dustin's, then?" Marcus said, walking into my apartment behind me. Marcus would have this conversation by himself until I spoke up. He wouldn't leave. That wasn't Marcus. He was persistent.

"Yeah. Micah's my nephew."

Marcus nodded and went and made himself comfortable on the couch.

"She giving you a hard time? If I remember right, you sure had a lot of interest in her back in the day. You got sent to alternative school for a month after beating the shit out of that guy who had cornered her in the hallway and was touching her while she tried to push him away. Broke the kid's nose."

Alternative school had sucked. It was for the thugs who screwed up so bad they took them out of the regular school and sent them to something like a boot camp. Luckily, there had been witnesses who vouched that the guy was touching Sienna inappropriately and that he'd taken two swings at me. One had actually given me a black eye, so it hadn't all been completely my fault. He'd done alternative school with a busted nose.

"She was a kid. She needed someone to take care of her. Too damn pretty for her own good."

Marcus let out a small laugh. "She was more than pretty, from what I remember, but she was Dustin's. Or so you always said. Although Dustin chose to ignore her for weeks until he finally saw just how much attention she was getting."

"Don't," I warned him. He knew I didn't let anyone talk bad about my brother. Ever. He'd been a kid and he'd made some bad decisions, but he'd had a good heart. And he'd been destined to be great.

Marcus sighed. "I loved Dustin. You know that. I wasn't talking bad about him. I'd never do that."

"I know," I replied. I was just being defensive because I'd almost fucked Sienna and all I could think about was going back and tasting her again.

"Sienna letting you get to know Micah?"

I nodded. She was being more than awesome about that. Letting him stay the night at my parents' had made my mother's year. She adored that kid, and she adored his mother.

Another reason I had to stay away from Sienna. I couldn't upset my mother. My dad would likely beat my ass. And I'd let him.

"You got feelings for her?" Marcus asked me.

I looked over at him and decided that I wasn't sure how to answer that. I had feelings for her because she was the mother of my nephew. I had feelings for her because she was a part of Dustin, part of a memory. But there was something else there.

Something that had always been there and I'd always pushed away because of Dustin. Something that scared me because I needed to stop it now.

"She's Micah's mother. I care about her and her safety."

Marcus nodded, and I knew he was remembering just how crazy I'd been about keeping her safe before Micah. Then the night my brother had finally made his move . . . I'd been so relieved I'd gotten trashed.

"You're one of the best men I know. You wear your tats and piercings and those damn leather bracelets that only you could get away with. But inside you are one big teddy bear. When someone you love needs you, there is nothing you won't do for them. When I needed you, you were always there. I've never questioned your heart. It's made of fucking gold, and we all know it. We laugh at your crude jokes and snide comments because we know they mean nothing. It's part of your shield. Underneath, I don't know many men that compare. You're one of the best, Dewayne. One of the best."

If he knew my thoughts about Sienna right now, he'd change his mind.

Chapter Twelve

Eight years ago . . .

SIENNA

"Hey, gorgeous. You seen Dewayne? He don't normally get too far from you," Preston Drake asked with a crooked smirk, his long blond hair tucked behind his ears. Most girls in school loved Preston. Not me. He was just funny. He made me smile, but he didn't make my heart race.

"Back off, Drake," Dewayne said as he sat down beside me on the picnic bench. He had just gotten back from alternative school and hadn't left my side. While he'd been gone, Marcus, Rock, and Preston had watched over me so closely that not many people spoke to me. Some girls did, like Marcus's sister, Amanda, and Rock's girlfriend, Trisha. But everyone else seemed intrigued and scared of me. It was frustrating.

"Knew you were around here somewhere," Preston said,

amused. "I've got some things to handle at home. I'm out of here. Let Marcus know I won't need a ride after school, yeah?" When he said the word "home," his easy smile had slipped and I'd seen anger or frustration there.

Dewayne nodded. "Sure. I'll tell him."

"See you tonight. Rock's place," he said, then shoved off from the table with a wink in my direction.

They were all very close and so different. But if one of them needed another, they were all there. Marcus was the one who stuck out like a sore thumb. Unlike the other three, he came from money. His daddy owned a lot of car dealerships, but you would never guess it from looking at Marcus.

"That all you're gonna eat?" Dewayne asked me.

It was nice to have someone to eat with me again. I had missed this. We didn't have the same lunch period, but somehow Dewayne always showed up at freshman lunch and kept me company. The past month I had sat alone. Sometimes Dustin would stop by and talk to me for a few minutes before the basketball team pulled him away to their table, but he never included me in that world.

I was losing Dustin. It hurt. He'd been my best friend for so long, it wasn't easy to watch him move further and further away from me. While Dewayne was gone, Dustin had almost seemed mad at me. As if it was my fault his brother had been sent to alternative school. I hadn't asked him to beat the crap out of that guy, but I had been thankful he'd stopped him.

"I'm not very hungry," I told him, which was a lie. My mother had decided I had gained weight lately, and she wanted to limit my food. I tried to explain it was my boobs, but she didn't accept that. She said my fat was going there and I needed to stop eating so much. She wasn't well endowed, and she believed I wouldn't be either if I ate less.

So I had an apple and some celery sticks for lunch. My waist had gotten smaller, but it was only making my boobs look even bigger. The bigger they looked, the more panicked my mother got and the less food she gave me.

"You've lost weight," Dewayne said. "Need to gain some more weight, Little Red."

"Hey, Sienna," Dustin said, setting his tray down on the other side of the table. Surprised, I looked up at him.

"Hey," I replied, happy to see him. I missed him.

"You look really good," he said, his eyes glancing down at my chest, then back up at my face with an approving grin.

"She always looks good," Dewayne informed him.

Dustin glanced at his brother and looked guilty. "Yeah, she does," he replied, then turned back to me. "I've been busy with things since school started, and I haven't been around a lot. I'm sorry about that."

I nodded. I understood his need to fit in with the team. It was what he loved, and I was just his friend. I had once hoped he would see me as something more, but he was Dustin Falco and I was just the girl next door. Not the head cheerleader or dance team captain. Both those girls had caught Dustin's attention. I'd seen him off in corners with them often.

"You want to go over and eat with me and the team?" Dustin asked, keeping his gaze on me and not looking at Dewayne.

I had been secretly wishing he would invite me into his new world with him, but I couldn't get up and leave Dewayne. He had been my friend when I didn't have one. Dewayne was beautiful and larger than life, and he made me feel special. Dustin had never made me feel special, at least not in the way I'd hoped.

"I—"

"It's about damn time," Dewayne said, interrupting me. Then he stood up. "Go eat with my brother. I think he's got his head out of his ass now. But if he sticks it back up his ass, you come tell me. I'll take care of you."

Then Dewayne Falco walked off. I sat there and watched him leave the cafeteria without a backward glance.

"Come on, Sienna. Let me introduce you to everyone. Most of them have been asking about you for a while now. Dewayne's made you pretty damn popular with the guys."

He had?

I stood up, took my meager lunch, and let Dustin lead me over to the popular table, where basketball players and cheerleaders gathered. The head cheerleader, who had been on Dustin's arm all last week, glared at me. I wanted to go back to the safety of Dewayne. Kimmy Bart was not someone I wanted as an enemy. She owned this school. She was also tall, thin, and blonde. Guys ogled her legs like they were the Holy Grail. And all that long blond hair made her look like an angel.

"Sienna, this is everyone. Everyone, this is my girl, Sienna Roy."

And just like that . . . I became Dustin Falco's girl.

Present day . . .

DEWAYNE

I hung up the phone with Momma after finding out she had Micah with her. Sienna had needed to work overtime and she'd called Momma to see if she would mind getting him from his after-school day care. Momma had been tickled pink that she got to keep him this afternoon.

I had turned my truck to the salon, and I was parked out back beside Sienna's car, waiting on her to get off work. We needed to talk, and I didn't want to do it at her house where Micah could come home or my momma could see I was over there alone with Sienna. She'd asked me five times already why I had been over there Saturday morning. Lying to my mother wasn't easy.

The back door opened and Hillary walked out. Shit. Not who I wanted to see. She looked at me and her eyes narrowed. Then she came my way. I hadn't seen Hillary since I'd gotten out of her bed after a one-nighter. She'd been drinking. I'd been drinking. And she had a really damn good body.

My window was already rolled down when she reached it.

"Leave her alone, Falco. She's a good girl. A sweet girl. And you"—she pointed at me—"ain't something that girl can deal with. She doesn't understand guys like you. I've watched her, and every man who walks into that place hits on her, and she ain't got a clue. Even Gretchen's clients can't keep their eyes off her. She's sweet. Too sweet. So crank this truck and get the hell out of here."

Not what I had been expecting. She wasn't out here to yell at me for running out on her after sex. She was warning me off Sienna. Interesting.

"She's the mother of my nephew, so I can't stay away from her. She's family."

Hillary's eyes went wide. Apparently, Sienna hadn't told them Micah was a Falco. Which was something that bothered me—I didn't like Dustin's boy not having his last name.

"Well, shit," she muttered. "I didn't know the kid was Dustin's."

I just nodded. The back door opened again, catching my attention, and Sienna stepped out. Her eyes immediately found my truck, and they shifted to Hillary at my door. Then she jerked her attention away from us and hurried across the parking lot to her beat-to-shit car.

"Move," I told Hillary before I swung my door open and headed after Sienna.

"Sienna, wait," I called out. She paused with her hand on the door handle. "I came here to see you," I explained, as if I had been doing something wrong. Jesus, I'd only kissed her. If I was here seeing Hillary, it would be perfectly fine. But for some reason it felt like I had been caught cheating.

She glanced back over her shoulder. "Why?"

"Because we need to talk. And not at your house," I said, and motioned to my truck. "Come for a ride with me."

She seemed unsure until her eyes followed Hillary, who was headed to her car. When Sienna looked back at me, she let out a weary sigh but walked toward me. "Okay," she said, and we walked side by side back to my truck.

I opened the passenger-side door and held out my hand to help her up, but she ignored it and climbed up on her own. Which made her sweet ass stick up in a very appealing way in those leggings she was wearing.

I closed the door, the image of her in those tight pants taunting me as I made my way over to my side of the truck. I climbed in and looked over at her. She was wearing sleeves that stopped just below her elbow. Still covering her bruise. Fuck me. "How's your arm?" I asked her.

"It's fading and it doesn't hurt anymore," she said with a smile that didn't meet her eyes.

"I'm a fuckup, Sienna. The bruise on your arm proves that. I shouldn't get to breathe the same air you do." I stopped myself before I said anything more. I wasn't ever going to get over that bruise. It was going to haunt me long after it faded away. "And I'm sorry. About the kiss. It was uncalled for, and I shouldn't have."

She tensed up beside me, but only for a moment. Then she relaxed her shoulders and crossed her legs, and damned if that wasn't fascinating. "Probably not a good idea. You're right."

So she agreed. We shouldn't have kissed. "I don't want things to get awkward with us."

She nodded. "Me neither."

"So, we can just be friends. Or family. We're family."

She nodded again.

She didn't feel like family. I watched as she tucked a strand of hair behind her ear, and I wanted to reach out and see if it was as silky as it looked. I'd missed that opportunity when I'd been eating her alive. My hands had gone from her face to her ass. I should have felt her hair.

"I know I'm, uh . . . not very experienced. I don't . . . I mean, Dustin was the only one I, uh . . . I did anything with. So I was curious. I haven't been kissed in a long time." She shut her mouth and closed her eyes tightly. She was trying to explain her reaction to me, but the fact that no one had touched her in six years was a little more information than I could handle.

How was she so untouched? I knew she'd said she didn't date, but, hell, how'd she get release? After having sex before, she'd want it, right? Need it?

"Not even any one-night stands or friends with benefits?" I asked.

She blushed and shook her head but wouldn't look at me.

"You don't need it?" *I* needed to shut the hell up. This was not a conversation you had with someone who was your "family."

She shrugged. "Not really. I mean . . . I never understood what the big deal was."

What? Holy hell. My sixteen-year-old brother hadn't been experienced enough to do it right, apparently.

"You've never had an orgasm?" I asked before I could stop myself.

Her blush deepened and she didn't respond.

Did that mean . . . she got herself off? Motherfucker! Why was I thinking about this? This was not helping me defuse my Sienna lust. The idea of slipping my hand into her panties and bringing her pleasure was so damn tempting.

"You do it yourself," I said, supplying the answer for her and knowing I needed to shut the hell up.

She pressed her lips together and closed her eyes tightly again. Bingo. She played with her pussy. Damn, that image was gonna give me some serious shower time later.

"Let's not talk about this, okay?" She reached for the door handle, but I wasn't ready to let her go. The desire to smell her was too much. I tugged her over to me and buried my head in her neck and inhaled. Fuck, she smelled good. So damn good. She also sounded good.

Her body leaned in to me and I wanted it. More.

"You smell good, baby. Real good. I bet that pussy smells even better," I whispered in a growl as I slid my hand between her legs. She let out a small cry.

Fuck, fuck, fuck. I wanted her. I wanted to hear her as she orgasmed. I wanted to see her play with herself. Was she bare, or were there curly red hairs down there to tease me?

"Dewayne?" she breathed, her chest rising and falling so fast that her cleavage taunted me. She'd always had the best damn tits.

"Yeah, baby?" I replied, running my nose up her neck.

"Gretchen is watching us," she said, and that was the wake-up call I needed. Shit. I had forgotten where we were.

I moved away from her, missing the smell and heat of her on my hand. I needed to get laid. She was screwing with my head. But first I wanted to go beat off to the image of her touching herself.

"I, we, this, um . . . I should go," she said, and moved away from me.

I couldn't argue. She should go before I gave in and attacked her again.

She opened the door, and I managed to remember what I had wanted to ask her. "Tomorrow night I'll bring dinner. I'd like to visit Micah," I said.

I didn't say I wanted to see her, but I did. I so fucking did.

She nodded. "Of course. You can take him out if you want to. You don't have to stay at my house. I trust you with him."

She was giving me an out. I wasn't taking it. As hard as it was getting to keep my hands off her, I wanted to see her too. "I'll bring dinner. And you'll eat more. Because nothing on your body is fucking average, Sienna. Understand that. You're perfect. Too damn perfect."

Her mouth opened slightly, and then she closed it and quickly got out of my truck. I sat there and watched her as she got into her car and buckled up. I waited until she pulled out of the parking lot before leaving. I didn't even look Gretchen's way.

Chapter Thirteen

SIENNA

"More," I whispered into the dark room. "Please, Dewayne, I want more. Do it harder," I begged. My eyes were closed tightly as Dewayne held his body over me, sliding in deeper and deeper. I lifted my legs up his back and buried my face in the pillow beside me as I cried out from how good he felt. How beautiful his body was as he worked over me. His naughty words told me how sexy I was and how good I felt.

I worked my fingers harder, letting the fantasy play out until my body shuddered with release. It was the same fantasy I had been using since Dewayne had walked into my house the first day we'd returned. It was getting more and more detailed. Like tonight, he'd told me I smelled good as he tasted me and ran his tongue where no one's had ever been.

I was getting worked up again and I needed to sleep. Fantasies of Dewayne could go on for hours. I had no shame in the darkness of my room. He was here with me, and I loved everything he did. When he'd asked me today if I pleasured myself, I was sure it was all over my face. I couldn't get away from him fast enough.

Him knowing he starred in my nightly playtime would be humiliating.

The fact that I got off on the fantasy of him inside me was interesting, since until Dewayne's return to my life I'd normally fantasized about other stuff. The act of actual intercourse had never held that appeal for me. But the idea of Dewayne being over me and between my legs made me hot and bothered. Maybe I was just old enough to enjoy it now. I'd been so young with Dustin.

My phone dinged and I reached for it. No one ever texted me this late.

Dewayne: You awake?

Why was he texting me? Oh God, had he known somehow that I had just used his body to pleasure myself?

I let my finger hover over the phone keys a moment, then finally gave in and replied.

Me: No
Dewayne: Are you in bed?

What was he asking that for?

Me: Yes

I should ignore this.

Dewayne: Do you sleep naked?

Okay. Wait a minute. This was not us being friendly. And I couldn't handle him doing this hot-and-cold stuff.

Me: What do you want? This conversation is going in a bad direction.

He didn't reply right away. I thought for a moment my scolding him had made him back off. Then my phone lit up again.

Dewayne: I know. I'm sorry.

That was it. Why did I feel so disappointed?

Dewayne: It's just if you're gonna play with yourself I want to know. I want to see it. Or at least you can tell me about it.

Holy crap. The tingling between my legs startled me. He was only texting me and I was reacting to him. I should turn off my phone and forget this conversation. Tomorrow he would regret it and push me away. He was probably drunk.

But maybe he wouldn't remember it . . . maybe.

Me: I've already taken care of that.

I pressed send before I could stop myself.

Dewayne: Motherfuck. Do it again. Tell me about it. Or let me FaceTime you and watch your face. God, let me watch your face.

Oh wow. He was drunk. He had to be. This was not careful Dewayne.

Me: I don't think that's a good idea.
Dewayne: I know it's a bad idea. But damn, Sienna, you're driving me crazy. I just want a little taste. If you'd spread those legs for me and let me taste you just once, then we could be friends. I just need a taste, baby. I know it's gonna be sweet.

Oh. My. God.
I stared at the phone in my hand and my whole body

trembled. Maybe I could FaceTime him. If he kept talking like this, I was going to beg him to come taste all he wanted.

Me: I don't know what to say.
Dewayne: Let me FaceTime you and watch you touch that
    pussy I want to fucking bury my face in.

I was a goner. This was too much. I wanted this, as dumb as it sounded.

Me: What happens tomorrow?
Dewayne: We keep being friends and forget we did this.
    Just give me this tonight. I need something. I've spent
    way too much time imagining it. I need visuals.

Okay. One time. I could do that. We would forget tomorrow.

Me: Okay.

My phone rang almost instantly. It was a FaceTime call from Dewayne Falco.

Oh shit. I couldn't believe I was going to do this. It was so bad. But exciting. And I trusted Dewayne. I had always trusted him.

"Hello," I said, looking into Dewayne's eyes. The glow of lamplight illuminated his face. I was in the dark.

"Turn on a light. I need to see you."

I wasn't wearing makeup, but I guess he'd seen me like this before. I reached over and turned on the lamp beside me.

"Fuck, that's better. So much better," he said in a pleased rumble.

I wasn't sure I could do this now. He wasn't hidden behind text messages anymore. He was right there in front of me.

"Are you sure we should do this?" I asked him, hoping he'd changed his mind and terrified he would at the same time.

"Take off your panties, Sienna," was his response.

"Okay," I replied, and reached down to take them off.

"I want to see," he said in a deep voice.

All right. I held the phone with one hand so he could see me taking my panties off with the other hand. I wasn't waxed completely. I did keep only a small strip of hair there because I hated how it felt when it was bare.

"Fuck, you got red curls," he muttered. "I want to bury my nose in that and inhale. So damn deep you stay with me for days after."

I whimpered. It was all I could do. All the naughty talking I had imagined in my fantasies was never this good. He was much better at it than my imaginary Dewayne was.

"Slip a finger in, baby. Let me watch."

I was so turned on I didn't even question him. I did as he told me, and knowing he was watching me made me moan with pleasure. It was almost as if it was him touching me.

"That's it. Fuck, that pussy is wet. I can see the curls all sticking together. That swollen clit needs attention. Give her some. Easy and slow," he said in a low growl.

I did exactly like he said.

"Easy . . . Fuck yeah. Now let me watch you suck that finger clean.

Oh my. I had never tasted myself. I wasn't sure I wanted to.

"Come on, Sienna. I need you to taste your sweet pussy for me. I want to eat it so damn bad. Do it so I can watch, baby. Do it for me."

When he said it like that, I was pretty sure I'd do anything. I held the phone back up to my face and watched his face as I slipped the finger into my mouth.

"Suck it, baby," he said, breathing heavy. Then I saw his arm moving.

"Are you . . . are you . . ." I couldn't even ask him.

"Yeah, Little Red, I'm fucking getting off on this. Best damn jerk I've ever had. Now let me see how wet you are."

Knowing he was enjoying this so much he was beating off, I opened my legs and held the phone down there so he could see exactly how turned on I was.

I heard him curse and groan. "Touch it for me. Fucking touch it. Damn plump pussy lips are the prettiest pink I've ever seen."

Yes, Dewayne was the king of dirty talk.

I slipped another finger down until my fingertip touched

the entrance I had been asking Dewayne to fuck harder just a little while ago.

"Fuck that pussy for me. God knows I want inside it so bad I can't think straight. It looks so tight. Almost fucking new. Touch it for me, baby."

I began pumping a finger in and out of me, and Dewayne's name left my mouth.

"Face. I want to see your face," Dewayne demanded.

I was lost in my fantasy, but I moved the phone back to my face, and the dark look in Dewayne's eyes made me tremble.

"Say my name again," he said as his arm pumped, causing his muscles to flex. He was gorgeous.

I cried out his name and threw my head back.

"Look in my eyes," he barked, and I did. I forced my eyes open and ran my finger over my clit just as I came apart. It was so much better than my earlier orgasm.

Dewayne's grunt and shout followed mine, and I smiled at the knowledge that he'd enjoyed watching me that much.

"Fuck," he breathed. "You're gonna ruin me. Fucking ruin me," he said in a low whisper.

I was breathing hard and didn't respond. The embarrassment that had left me when I had gotten so worked up came back. The knowledge that he had gotten off too helped marginally. At least I hadn't been alone in that.

"Tomorrow we're just friends," he reminded me, and

although I knew that, hearing him say it hurt. It hurt bad. Because all I could think about now was doing that for real. He apparently wasn't thinking the same thing.

"Right," I agreed.

"You good?" he asked, looking worried.

I was sure my disappointment was all over my face. I had to cover that up, and fast. "Yeah. More than. I need sleep now. So . . . uh . . . thanks," I said with a forced smile.

He nodded but didn't look convinced. "Yeah, okay. I'll see you tomorrow."

"See you then. Good night," I replied, and ended the call before he could respond.

DEWAYNE

What had I done? How was I supposed to forget that? Fuck it all, seeing Sienna play with herself wasn't something I needed to see. Now I was all screwed up in the head. My attraction to her was now full-blown need. I needed to eat her needy little pussy. And it was pretty. So damn pretty and plump. And pink.

Damn! I had made a major mistake. I could not have Sienna that way. Ever. She was Micah's mother. She needed a man who was worthy of her. Not me. I wasn't what she needed. I had too much baggage. Besides, what happened after I fucked her and was done? I was always over a woman once I fucked her. The mystery was gone and I was finished. I couldn't do that to Sienna.

I guess it was a good thing that when I cracked I did it through FaceTime. That was just playtime. Nothing too serious. Sienna couldn't get all googly-eyed with me. She still had Mr. Vice Principal to date.

He'd just better keep his hands off her.

Fuck. I was fucked. I had to shake this loose. Without fucking her out of my system.

I revisited the memory of her slipping her finger into her mouth, and my dick went from zero to sixty. I had to get laid, and fast. Before I screwed up seriously bad. My parents would never forgive me, I would never forgive me, and Sienna would hate me. I couldn't lose Micah because I wanted in between his momma's legs.

They were really great legs. Fucking amazing legs. The skin on the inside of her thighs looked so soft. Shit. I wanted a taste. Maybe I could get a taste of her on my tongue, and then I'd be over her. Then she wouldn't hate me. I'd explain that it was just for fun. Nothing more.

I walked up to her front door with burgers and fries from the Pickle Shack. I had to get a grip on this. Tonight was about Micah. Not Sienna and her hot little body. If she had a magic pussy, then I didn't need to get near it. I'd seen my friends come in contact with magic pussy, and I wasn't ready for that shit. Ever.

"Dewayne!" Micah cheered as he opened the door. He had known I was coming, and he was still excited to see me. That helped remind me why I was here.

"Hey, little man. Ready for the best burgers you've ever eaten?" I asked him.

He frowned. "Do they have mac 'n' cheese on them?"

The kid was obsessed with mac 'n' cheese. And as a matter of fact, I'd had mac 'n' cheese added to his burger.

"Yours does," I told him. His little eyes went wide and his grin got wider.

"YAY! Momma, Dewayne got me a burger with mac 'n' cheese on it!"

I looked up just as Sienna walked into the living room from the kitchen. She was wearing another pair of leggings and a baggy T-shirt over them. No makeup and her hair was up in a ponytail. If this was her trying not to act like she wanted to impress me, then she didn't know me that well. Because her looking all comfortable and clean was sexy as hell.

"He has you all figured out," Sienna said, smiling down at Micah before looking up at me.

She smiled at me shyly and had that look women got when they wanted something more. Shit! Shit! Shit! I had told her we were just friends. That what we'd done didn't change anything.

"Um, you two can go ahead and eat. I've already eaten, and I'm going to go take a soak in the tub. Enjoy your visit."

Or maybe not. She was escaping. I didn't want her to escape. I wanted to hear her laugh and see her eyes light up. I also wanted to make her smile. And see her eat. Dammit.

"You don't like burgers?" I asked, trying to think of a way to keep her in here.

"She loves 'em," Micah offered.

"I got you the best," I told her.

She looked like she wanted some but was fighting it. Was it because she couldn't look at me? I didn't like that. I wanted her comfortable with me.

"You didn't eat nothing but a few pretzels with peanut butter, Momma."

The kid was telling on her. Which was funny and was giving me leverage.

"You don't have to eat the whole thing, just eat some. I know you don't eat a lot."

Micah looked up at me with wide eyes. "Yeah, she does! She can eat lots more than me. She normally eats a whole burger, fries, and a piece of pie."

Then why the hell had she picked at the pizza? Was it really because of the "average" comment? I'd straightened that out already. Hell, after last night she shouldn't have any concerns around me.

"Gotta keep those curves in place. It'd be a shame for them to disappear," I told her.

"What curves?" Micah asked.

Her eyes went wide. She looked over at the bags in my hand and let out a sigh, then smiled. "Okay. I'll eat. It smells delicious."

Score.

Micah started telling me about his day at school, and I tried like hell to listen to him and not focus on his mother sitting down across from me, eating her burger like it was the best thing she'd ever put in her mouth. She'd clearly been starving, from the way she was eating. I hated that she'd picked at her pizza the other night and had been hungry. All because of my dumbass comment to my mother.

"And Mama T said I could come over to her house and stay the night again soon. We're out of school Friday and Mama T said I could stay with her 'cause I don't want to stay at day care. Her and Grandpa Dave's house is funner."

"More fun," Sienna corrected him.

"Yeah, more fun, and so maybe I could stay the night tomorrow night. I told Momma, but she said she'd have to talk to Mama T first."

I had no doubt my mother would take Micah any time he wanted her to. My dad, too. When Micah had called him Grandpa Dave the other day, he'd had to leave the room because he'd teared up. My dad wasn't a crier. Seeing him get emotional like that wasn't something I was used to. Once again it made me feel like I owed Sienna Roy the world. She'd been alone and scared, but she'd had Dustin's baby anyway and she'd been a damn good mom. All on her own. Micah was the healing I didn't think my parents would ever find. And all because one young girl was brave enough to be a mother without a family's support around her.

My chest ached and something fierce settled in. I had to protect this woman. Even if I was protecting her from myself. I wanted her to have nothing but happiness in life. She deserved that. More than anyone else I knew, Sienna Roy deserved the best life had to offer.

And the best wasn't me.

"And I bet that Momma could go on another date with Mr. Dodge." Micah's comment snapped me out of my thoughts.

"Mr. Dodge hasn't asked me out again, Micah," Sienna said to her son while setting drinks down in front of us.

"Then he's an idiot," I said. The dude had stepped way up out of his league with Sienna.

Sienna laughed. "I think he might have seen a side of me he wasn't crazy about."

She was referring to our argument in the parking lot. She'd been all fired up and gorgeous that night. I couldn't even remember it fondly, though, because the memory of my hurting her arm was too painful. I hated myself for that.

"Then Uncle Dewayne can take you out on a date. You think Momma is pretty, don't you?" Micah said, and I watched Sienna freeze.

A panicked look came over her face, and then she looked at me. I wasn't sure what to say to the kid. I thought his momma was gorgeous, but I didn't think saying that would help get him off this idea.

"Um, well, see, Uncle Dewayne is family. You don't date family," Sienna said to Micah, and took a seat across from him.

Micah frowned, then shrugged. Luckily, he let it go while he took a bite of his burger.

"How's the mac 'n' cheese burger?" I asked him, wanting to ease the sudden awkward silence.

Micah gave me a thumbs-up.

"I can't believe you got them to put mac 'n' cheese on the burger," Sienna said with an amused smile.

"My boy wants a mac 'n' cheese burger, he's gonna get one," I told her.

There was a flash of something in her eyes, and then she looked down at her own burger and studied it a moment before she picked it up and bit into it.

I wasn't sure what I'd said, but she got quiet after that. Micah didn't. He started telling me all about the Heat's lineup this year and how they were going to beat each team. Or how Chris Bosh was going to beat each team. I didn't have anything to add to the conversation because basketball had never been my sport. But I listened.

Chapter Fourteen

SIENNA

After I finished my burger, I excused myself and went to the safety of my bedroom while Micah took Dewayne to the living room to make him watch *Return of the Jedi*. It was a school night, and I knew Micah would end up falling asleep twenty minutes into the movie. He was like clockwork with his sleeping pattern. The kid required serious sleep.

I would need to be out of the bath and dressed when Dewayne left, so I could make sure Micah was tucked into bed. I sat down on the bed and reached for my phone. It was time I made a call.

I'd been putting off calling my aunt Cathy for two reasons. One, I wanted to see if she'd ever call me and check in on us. She hadn't. Two, I was thankful for Aunt Cathy's willingness to let me live in her house for so long, and I didn't want to hear she'd had anything to do with the Falcos not getting my letters. But I honestly didn't see any other explanation. I had resigned myself to the fact that she had taken them.

I scrolled down the list of numbers in my phone until I found hers, and then I pressed send. When I had told Aunt Cathy I was moving, she hadn't seemed to care either way. She was glad my mother had finally stepped up to help me, but that was about it. No warm hugs or any other emotions.

"Hello?" Aunt Cathy's familiar voice came over the line.

"Hey, Aunt Cathy, it's Sienna," I said.

"Good to hear from you, Sienna. I take it life there is good?"

She was always so formal. Even with Micah she had been stern and strict. She didn't do nonsense of any kind. She reminded me a lot of my dad, even though she's my mother's sister.

"Yes, ma'am. It's good here. Micah likes his new school, and I am doing well at my job. Micah, uh, met the Falcos. They didn't know about him until they met him. Now they're very active in his life."

I stopped and waited for her to say something. She didn't.

"I sent letters to them. So many letters. I wanted and needed them to know about Micah. Micah needed them. Tabby is the wonderful grandmother I knew she would be. Micah missed that for five years of his life. I don't understand how this happened."

Again I was met with silence. I started to say something else, but my aunt finally spoke up. "If you are calling me to ask me if I took those letters, this is a conversation you need to be having with your mother. I've done her job long enough, Sienna. I didn't have children because I didn't want the responsibility. Yet my younger sister neglected her responsibility to her own child, so I stepped in until you could stand on your own two feet. However, I'm not your mother. What happened with those letters is something I don't have to answer for. You were staying in my house. I could do whatever I pleased. You need to call your mother and have a talk with her. It's past time. Now, if that is all you'd like to talk about, I have some work to do."

There was nothing else to say. Aunt Cathy had made it very clear. "No, ma'am, that's it. I'll let you get back to work," I replied.

"You're a smart girl, Sienna. Use that brain of yours and make a life that kid you were determined to have deserves. Let the past be the past." And with that, Aunt Cathy hung up the phone.

I wasn't surprised. Not really. She'd always been that way. Not once had she cooed over or cuddled Micah. She had treated us as if she was our warden, and now I realized that was really all she ever had been. But I'd been so desperate for someone to love us that I'd accepted whatever she was willing to give.

I looked out the window at the Falcos' across the street. They loved us. More important, they loved Micah. Maybe it was time I called my mother. I had to forgive her and forget the past. If she wanted to see Micah, who was I to keep her from him? He loved having family. He deserved it.

A knock on the bedroom door stopped me from calling her. I put the phone down, walked over, and opened it up to Dewayne holding a sleeping Micah.

"You want to change him before you put him in bed?" he asked in a whisper.

I nodded. "Take him to his room and lay him on the bed. I'll take it from there."

Dewayne did as instructed. I followed him to Micah's room, and then he stepped out while I took my time changing Micah into his pajamas. I kept waiting for the sound of the front door closing, but it wasn't happening. Which meant Dewayne was waiting on me. When I couldn't do anything else, I tucked Micah in and slipped quietly from his room.

Dewayne was standing in the living room with his arms crossed over his chest, staring at the pictures of Micah and me I had lining the mantel. One was from the day he learned to take his first steps. Another was from his third birthday. The last one was taken the day I graduated from beauty school.

"You were just a kid here," he said, picking up the photo of me and Micah when he'd taken his first steps.

"I was almost eighteen," I said. But I had been a kid.

"You look so proud of him. You don't look tired or bitter. Just happy."

"I *was* happy. My baby boy was walking, and I was the only person he would walk to. He was trying to follow me around the house. That's how he started walking. Crawling wasn't fast enough."

Dewayne set it back down. "Do you have extras? I'd like photos of him and you. My mom and dad would too."

I had taken so many photos and sent them with the missing letters. I'd also been keeping a scrapbook for my parents up until he was three, but then I realized they were never going to reach out and get to know Micah. So I'd stopped making it. But I still had it.

"I have a scrapbook of his first three years that y'all can have. I can get you copies of photos from the past two years to add to it."

Dewayne smiled. "That would be great. I want to see him as he grows. I want to see you with him. I love watching the way he looks at you. It says a lot about you and what kind of mother you are. That kid thinks you can do no wrong. He tells my mom and dad all about the things you've taken him to do and the things you cook that he loves. I think Momma may love you more than she loves me these days."

He grinned when he said it. That was the only reason I knew he was kidding. I didn't want to make him feel like I was trying to walk into his life and change it. I just wanted Micah to know him. Micah already loved him.

"Your mother loves you," I said, assuring him.

He chuckled and nodded. "Yeah, she does. Don't know why."

Because you're lovable and kind. Because you make everyone around you smile. Because you have a really big heart. I remember you taking the time to make a scared little fourteen-year-old girl feel safe in high school. I didn't say any of those things, though. I couldn't. Not now. Not after last night.

"You're blushing. You thinking about last night?" he said with a wicked gleam in his eyes.

I covered my warm cheeks with my hands, hating my tendency to blush.

"It's okay. I can't seem to stop thinking about it either."

Oh my. The silly flip my heart always did around him turned into a wild flutter.

"Problem is, I got to stop thinking about it. You do too. We can't go there. We have Micah to think about, and I don't do relationships, Sienna. It's not me. I'm my own man. I don't like to be tied down. I don't even want to think of settling down. Being the man you deserve. It's not me. You need the settling-down type. You need a Cam Dodge in your life. Not me. Us," he said, motioning his hand between the two of us, "we're friends. Hell, we're family. That boy in there is what's important, and we both love him. Let's not mess up what he needs with something that won't end well."

The fluttering stopped. It sank to my stomach and formed a tight, painful knot. He was making sure I got that he wasn't interested in something with me. Just some phone sex and he was ready to move on. That hurt way more than the "average" comment he'd said he hadn't meant.

"You understand, right? It ain't that you aren't gorgeous. You'll make a man a really lucky sonuvabitch one day. I'm just not the man you settle down with. I'm the bad boy girls sew their wild oats with. But I'll be the best damn uncle in the world. And if you need anything, you come to me. I'll take care of it. Always."

He would do anything for me because of Micah. That was it. If it weren't for Micah, he wouldn't care that I was back. That I existed. I was a young single mom with a job that got me by from week to week. I didn't have a lot to offer someone. I got that. But hearing Dewayne say I wasn't enough hit me hard. Really hard.

I just nodded. I couldn't speak.

He smiled, walked over, and pressed a kiss to my forehead like I was a kid. Then he turned and left.

I stood there for a long time. Letting it all sink in. Tomorrow I would move on. Tomorrow I would find a way to forget Dewayne Falco. But right now I wasn't ready.

DEWAYNE

By Thursday I had stayed away from Sienna's for a week. I had texted Sienna and told her to take Micah to my parents' Saturday morning, that I would pick him up there. I had spent the day with him, then left him with my parents minutes before Sienna got back, using my job as an excuse for running off.

I was trying to give myself time to forget how much I wanted her. She had been so accepting of my reasons for not being able to be with her that it had been painful. I wasn't sure what I had wanted her to do. Argue with me? Maybe. Maybe I wanted a reason to kiss her lips again. Touch her in places I'd dreamed about. Fuck. Who was I kidding? I loved being near her. Watching her move. She had this way about her. Even when she was doing something simple, I was completely fascinated by her.

She had listened to my reasons and then nodded. That was it. Nothing else. So I'd run out of there and hadn't been back. I couldn't face her. Because I was pretty damn sure I'd grab her and kiss her until we both forgot what a bad idea that all was.

I took a drink of my Coke and fought the urge to light up a cigarette. Not drinking or smoking was fucking kicking my ass. When I had turned down a beer and ordered a Coke, Rock had looked at me like I'd lost my mind. He didn't understand. He had never laid a hand on Trisha that wasn't a hand she wanted there.

"Preston's alone. That's odd," Rock said as he took a drink of his cold, foamy beer. I was lusting over his drink. Shit.

The pretty boy in our group pulled out a stool and sat down with a grin. He was engaged and happy about it. Real happy. He was always smiling. Asshole.

"Where's Manda?" Rock asked.

"She finally shake you loose?" I asked.

Preston shot me an annoyed glare. "No. She's coming. She's bringing a friend," he said, then grinned again.

"Stop smiling so damn much. Hurts my eyes," I grumbled, and took another drink of my Coke.

"Ignore him. That Coke he's drinking is straight-up Coke. Nothing added. He's sober and surly," Rock explained.

Preston's eyebrows shot up about the same time Rose Mann walked up beside me, wrapped her arm around my shoulders, and gave me a good view down her shirt. I'd known Rose since high school. We all had. She'd moved into town when we were sophomores, and she immediately made the cheerleading squad. I'd fucked her back then, but only once. Hadn't touched her since.

Still, she had aged well. Still had perky tits and a head of brown curls. "Hello, Rose," I said, sliding my arm around her waist and pulling her closer.

"Hello to you, Falco," she purred, and pressed against me. She then moved her gaze over to Preston. "You leave the fiancée behind tonight?"

Preston shook his head. "Don't let her too far out of my sight. She's headed this way soon."

Rose rolled her eyes, then glanced over at Rock. "And where's your little missus?"

"Be careful, Rose. We both know his little missus will take your ass out if you attempt to flirt with her man. You know better than to get near what belongs to Trisha."

The whole table laughed but Rose. Back in high school Rose had made a play for Rock after Preston had fucked her and tossed her aside. Trisha had slammed her against the lockers, broken several of her nails, and taken out a handful of her hair. No one hit on Rock after that.

"Whatever," Rose said, then laid her hand on my chest. "I'm here for *you*, anyway," she informed me. I was trying to decide if I wanted to give this a go tonight or not. I needed to do something to get Sienna out of my head. Rose was hot, but she was also a little crazy. I wasn't sure if I wanted to mess with crazy.

"There's my girl," Preston said. I swung my eyes over to see Amanda, and they collided with Sienna. Who was looking at Rose. Shit.

"Hey, Sienna. Glad you could make it," Preston said, getting up to pull out a stool for Sienna right beside me. "We won't make you sit on Dewayne's lap, seeing as it's already full of Rose. You can have a stool. It's more comfortable anyway." I watched as Sienna tore her gaze from Rose and forced a smile for Preston. Then she looked at me. She was on the verge of bolting. I could see it. Preston had known who Amanda was bringing and he hadn't told me. I was going to kick his ass.

"It's okay. If they start doing gross shit at the table, Rock will make them take it outside," Preston told her, then smirked at me. Dipshit.

Sienna walked over to the stool beside me like she was walking the plank. Slow and unsure.

"Who's this?" Rose asked, leaning over me and wrapping

her arm around me possessively, which pissed me off. She was trying to mark her territory, like she had any. I wasn't sure I wanted to spend the evening with her or not. I hadn't made up my mind yet.

"Sienna, this is Rose Mann," Amanda piped up in a sweet tone that she didn't mean. "She was older than you in school. She would have been . . . a senior your freshman year, I think." The comment about Rose being older had been a jab, but coming from sweet Amanda, who was in the safety of Preston Drake's arms, she was untouchable, and she knew it.

Sienna smiled at Rose. "I didn't know many people in school. I kind of blended into the crowd." That was Sienna's way of saying she didn't know who Rose was. But it was also bullshit. Sienna had never blended into anything.

"Sienna Roy? You were Dustin's girlfriend," Rose said, recognizing the name.

Sienna nodded and forced a smile, then turned away from me and looked at the band onstage. Jackdown wasn't up there yet. They didn't take the stage for another hour. A new band from Mississippi was playing right now.

"I thought you lost your mind and they shipped you off to a loony house."

Sienna flinched, and her shoulders went stiff. That was it. She'd come in here with Amanda, and I was pretty damn sure this was something she hadn't done in a long time. Rose wasn't going to ruin it for her. Even if having Rose in my lap kept my hands off Sienna.

I dropped the leg Rose was leaning on and moved my hand from her waist. She stumbled and had to grab the table to keep from falling on her face. "That'll be all. You can go now," I told her.

Amanda covered her giggle, and Rose glared at me. "What's your problem?"

"Obnoxious women who don't have shit for brains. So please be on your way," I replied with a bored drawl.

Preston cleared his throat to cover up his laugh. "Probably said the wrong thing, Rose. Best get going before he gets mad. He isn't drinking tonight, so he's a loose cannon."

Rose called me a jackass, then spun around and stalked off.

I waited until she was far enough away before I looked down at Sienna. She was studying me. The tension in her shoulders was gone. That was good.

"Sorry about that," I said, and she nodded.

Then she looked away again, back toward the stage.

I had to make some small talk because right now Preston and Rock were both trying to figure out what the hell was going on. But even I wasn't sure what was going on at the moment.

I opened my mouth to say something just as the band started up, and Sienna began swaying in her seat slightly. She liked to dance. I didn't dance. I hated dancing. I had to be drunk off my ass to dance, and even then I only did it if my partner and I were going from dancing to fucking.

But seeing Sienna sway in her seat with that smile on her face while she watched the people on the dance floor made me stand up and hold out my hand.

"Come on. Let's dance," I said. I knew I had just surprised the entire table, but I kept my focus on Sienna.

She beamed at me and slipped her hand in mine. The little black dress she was wearing with her cowboy boots made me want to pull her close so every man in here knew she was with me. Even if she wasn't.

"I didn't know you danced," she said.

"He don't," Preston said.

I didn't acknowledge this comment. I led her out onto the dance floor and pulled her into my arms, and it felt right.

So fucking right.

Chapter Fifteen

SIENNA

Dewayne's big body holding me close was better than the dancing. And I loved dancing. I had never been held close like this and danced with the right way. I kept inhaling Dewayne's masculine scent. He had a woodsy smell with a hint of peppermint.

He had glared so fiercely at the few people who had bumped into me on the crowded dance floor that no one was getting near us now. He also had me so close to him that I felt like we were one person. The music went from slow to more of a sexy beat, and I slipped my hands up to his shoulders and moved my hips to the music, letting my head fall back and closing my eyes. This was nice. Or more like fantastic. Dewayne's hands tightened on my hips, and I loved how possessed it made me feel. Even if we were just dancing. For this one moment I was his. And I loved it.

His leg moved between mine and I rubbed against him, only to freeze from the contact and inhale sharply. He was so much taller than me that the friction hit me in just the right place. I gripped the front of his shirt tightly in my fists. We were on a dance floor and I could not hump his leg. But all I had to do was move my hips a little and I'd feel that heavenly pressure again.

His hand was in mine, and he was pulling me from the dance floor before I could decide what to do next. I thought he was mad at me and we were going back to the table, but when I looked around, we were headed the opposite way. It looked like we were headed to a back door. Was that a bathroom? What was he doing?

Dewayne shoved people out of his way who didn't move on their own, and then he was slamming open the door and we were outside in the dark. There were no parking lot lights, only woods.

"Spread your legs, Sienna," he ordered as he pressed me up against the wall. "Pull up your skirt and open your legs," he said again, this time with a growl.

I was too startled to argue. He looked like he wanted what I wanted, so I did exactly like he said. I tugged up my dress and opened my legs.

Then his hand was there, cupping me as he breathed heavily. "This . . . we shouldn't do this. I'm not that guy. You remember I told you I'm not that guy. But I don't fucking dance,

Sienna. Do you understand me? I don't fucking dance."

I was confused. He had danced with me. He slid his finger inside my panties and I didn't care anymore. I grabbed his arms and cried out in relief and pleasure. He was actually touching me. This was real. And if I was asleep, I really didn't want to wake up.

"So wet," he said, pressing his lips to my neck. "Slick little hot pussy is gonna kill me. You are too much. I want a taste of you, and I can't keep my hands off you even though I know this will hurt you. I don't want to hurt you."

He wasn't hurting me now. I could hardly form words as he slid his finger inside my entrance. I squeezed his arms and panted.

"I want to fuck this. I want you. I want inside you. Right motherfucking now I want inside you so damn bad my dick is about to bust out of these jeans. But that will be all it is. We won't do it again. I don't do relationships. I don't want you hurt."

He wanted to fuck me. Just this once and then he'd be done with me. We would be friends again. Or he'd just be my son's uncle. Could I live with that? Could I give myself to him knowing it was just this once?

No.

I wanted more.

I'd loved Dustin when I had slept with him. Maybe I hadn't been in love with him, but a part of me did love Dustin. I hadn't been ready for sex then, but I had loved him and he had wanted to. He had loved me, and that had been enough. But this wasn't love with Dewayne. He didn't love me. He never would.

His finger slid back out of me, then circled my clit, and it felt so very good. Being with him would be the most epic moment of my life. I knew that. But then what? I would find a way to move on? Love someone else? Could I ever love someone else? If I tied myself to Dewayne this way, I wouldn't be able to let him go. Not in my heart. And didn't I deserve to be loved? To know what it felt like to be held like Preston held Amanda? To know that the man beside me wanted only me?

He was right. I deserved more.

I pushed him away, and he went without a fight. Closing my eyes, I caught my breath. "I want more. I can't. I can't do this with you and have it mean nothing to you. If you're going to walk away from me, then I can't do it. I'll want more. I don't want a taste of something I can never have."

I opened my eyes. Dewayne's hands were tucked in his pockets, and he hung his head as he took deep breaths. He looked defeated. I felt defeated. The young girl inside me who thought Dewayne Falco was my own prince charming was realizing he wasn't. He was a man. Just like any other.

"I'm sorry, so fucking sorry," he said, still not looking at me.

This was it. I couldn't go back inside. Not after he had hauled me out of there like that. I would call Amanda and apologize later. Right now I just wanted to go home.

I didn't tell him good-bye. I'd see him again soon enough. He would come see Micah. I would pretend like I didn't feel something for him. I would act as if he hadn't hurt me. I would deal. I was good at surviving. I could survive this.

Luckily, Amanda had driven to Live Bay with me, so I had my car here. Preston had dropped her off at my house earlier, and she'd helped me get dressed. She wouldn't need me to give her a ride. I climbed in my car and turned it toward home. To put on my pajamas and cuddle on the couch with the little boy there who loved me. The one man in my life who I would be enough for. I always had my son.

I was still three miles from home when the car started jerking. This had happened once before and I had managed to crank it back up after it went dead. I just didn't need it to happen now, on a dark road.

I pulled the car over to the side of the road just as it gave up the struggle. I waited a few minutes and tried starting it up, but it was completely dead. I couldn't sit here all night. I had to move. Besides, I had walked three miles home before. Maybe not at night, but I had walked three miles.

I grabbed my purse and took my keys with me, then headed the rest of the way home on foot. My feet were going to have blisters after walking three miles in these boots. That was the least of my problems, though. In the morning I had to find a tow truck service I could afford.

DEWAYNE

I didn't go back inside after she walked away. Instead, I leaned against the wall and laid my head back as her words returned to me in a rush. She wanted more. She wasn't willing to let me take her and have that be it.

She knew her self-worth. She didn't do casual sex. She respected her body. She was fucking perfect. I'd actually told her I didn't do relationships and that what we were doing was a fuck and nothing more. What kind of sorry motherfucker does that to a woman like Sienna?

Touching her had been . . . God . . . it had been amazing. She smelled even better than I'd imagined. I could still smell her on my hand. It was reminding me of what I wasn't good enough for. Dancing with her and feeling her body against mine had worked me into a frenzy. One only Sienna Roy could satisfy.

No one in that club appealed to me.

I didn't dance, but I had held her in my arms, and there I was, dancing with her. Holding her close. Enjoying every minute of it. Then she'd moved against my leg and trembled in my arms, and all I could think of was touching her. Making her come on my hand. Watching her.

I sank down to the ground and sat there. Songs played inside, and I could hear when Jackdown took the stage. The crowd roared, and I closed my eyes and wished like hell I had been stronger. Better.

"You gonna sit out here all night and beat yourself up for whatever the hell you did, or get up and go check on her?"

I opened my eyes to see Rock standing over me.

"She doesn't want to see me," I told him.

Rock cocked an eyebrow. "Really? 'Cause the girl I met inside looked at you like you were some angel from heaven. For a minute there I thought you might walk on fucking water."

Normally, a comment like that would've made me laugh. But right now I felt sick to my stomach. "She left. I told her all I'd ever be was a one-time fuck, and she said she wanted more. That she deserved more. And she's right. So I let her go."

Rock didn't respond right away. He agreed with her, I was sure. Everyone saw how amazing she was. It was easy to see.

"I've known you all my life. And I've never seen you treat anyone the way you treat Sienna. Not when we were in high school and not now. She's your one. The one who reaches you. The one who makes you different."

"She was Dustin's," I said, reminding him that in high school she was never mine. I had protected her when my brother hadn't. Nothing more.

"No one was ever Dustin's one. We both know that. I believe Sienna may be the only one who doesn't know that."

"Don't. He loved her. He made mistakes. He was a kid."

Rock shook his head. "It's time you faced some things. One of those things is that Dustin never deserved Sienna. You did. You gave her to him. She wanted you, and you handed her to him."

"She was a kid!" I yelled. I didn't want to hear this. Dustin had loved that girl. He had since he was little. He'd made some mistakes, but he'd have done anything to protect Sienna.

"Explain Kimmy Bart, then. Make it make sense in your head. Because it never has in mine," Rock said, then turned and walked away.

I watched him leave. I hated that he had brought up Kimmy Bart. I didn't want to think about her. I didn't want to remember what she'd done to my family. The pain she'd caused when we hadn't needed it.

She'd been one of Dustin's biggest mistakes. One I'd never wanted Sienna to know about. It would destroy her.

When I finally got up and went to my truck, I decided I'd drive by Sienna's to make sure her car was parked in the driveway. I would sleep better knowing she was home safe. I should have followed her since she was upset, but I had needed space and time to think first.

My headlights illuminated a car pulled off to the side of the road, and my heart stopped. It was Sienna's. Shit! I slammed on my brakes and jumped out of the truck, but Sienna wasn't in the car. I grabbed my phone out of my pocket and dialed her number while I jumped back in my truck and searched for her on the side of the road.

It went to voice mail.

Shit.

I'd started to dial her number again when a text lit up my screen.

Sienna: I'm in bed. I don't feel like talking tonight.

So she was home. Who had she called?

Me: I found your car. How did you get home?
Sienna: I walked.

Shit! That was at least three miles in the dark. Anything could have happened to her.

Me: Why didn't you call me?

She should have called me. She had my number. I'd told her if she ever needed me to call me.

Sienna: I needed space from you. I made it home okay.
Thanks for checking.

I dropped the phone to the seat beside me and drove by her house just to be sure she was okay. Then I called my dad to tell him to keep an eye on her because she didn't have a car.

After that I called Jimbo down at the wrecker service and paid him extra to get his ass out of bed and come tow that piece of shit to the junkyard. I told him I'd come get everything out of it in the morning.

Sienna was getting a new car. A safe car. Because I wasn't giving her an option. I intended to buy her and Micah a decent car. She'd never walk home in the dark ever again.

Chapter Sixteen

SIENNA

Tabby had brought Micah home the next morning to see me before I had to go to work. She'd said that Dewayne had said to let me know he'd had my car hauled off to the shop last night. He would be bringing my things by later and said not to worry about it. She'd also said that when I was ready to leave I should bring Micah back over and take her car. She wouldn't be needing it.

Micah had been telling me about his time with Mama T and Grandpa Dave ever since she'd left, so I hadn't had a chance to decide what I thought about Dewayne handling my car problem. On one hand, him having it towed was helpful, but I didn't have an unlimited budget. I'd planned to shop around for the cheapest rate.

"Did you know that Mama T and Grandpa Dave have pictures of you when you was little? I saw them last night, and you used to have lots of freckles. Did you get them erased?"

I laughed and pulled Micah onto my lap and cuddled with him. "They faded as I got older and I stopped running around outside all the time."

Micah slipped his little arms around me. "You smell good, Momma. I missed you."

I kissed the top of his head. "I missed you, too, Ace. So much."

"Mama T said Uncle Dewayne may be coming over today. Think he'll throw the football with me?"

I ran my hand over his silky hair. "I'm sure he will. Your Uncle Dewayne loves you." That was something I was sure of.

"When you get off work tonight, are we gonna have a movie night?"

"Yes, we are. Is it a Jedi night, or will we be pirates?"

He tilted his head back and smiled up at me. "We can be pirates. I know you like Captain Jack."

I laughed and tickled him while he giggled and squirmed.

"Momma. Hey, Momma," he said when he caught his breath. "I heard Mama T tell Grandpa Dave that she wished my last name was Falco like Daddy's."

I froze. Once, I had wanted that too. But now I wasn't sure. Everyone would know then. Was I ready for that?

"I like having the same last name as you. I don't wanna change it," he said, looking concerned.

I pulled him back into my arms in a hug. "If you want to be a Roy, then you can be," I told him. "But even if your last name isn't Falco, you're a Falco, kiddo."

He wrapped his arms around my neck. "I want to be what you are."

I held him close and breathed him in. He didn't have that baby smell anymore, and I missed it. But my little boy was growing up. Every day I saw more of his father in him.

"I love you, Micah," I told him.

"I love you more, Momma."

Not getting enough sleep last night was weighing on me. I was exhausted, and I had three blisters on my feet, which wasn't helping. It was getting harder to cover up my yawns. Hillary had caught me yawning twice already. I knew she didn't like me looking like I had partied hard all night. If she only knew the truth. I would explain about my car so she would at least know the reason I was obviously tired. I didn't want her thinking this was from a night of partying.

"You got a customer, Sienna," Gretchen called out. I turned around to see Cam Dodge dressed in his dress shirt and tie. I hadn't expected to see him again, much less coming in for a haircut.

"Okay, I'm free for the next hour," I said, and smiled at Cam. His grin looked somewhat apologetic. I don't know why. He had nothing to be sorry over. We had gone out once. No big deal that it had been almost two weeks ago.

"I need a trim," he said, walking toward me. I motioned for him to take a seat in my chair, and then I put a cape over him and fastened it around his neck.

"Your current hairdresser unavailable?" I asked.

He gave me that crooked grin that made him cute. "I normally go to the barber shop. You're easier on the eyes than Bill."

Smiling, I reached for a comb and checked out his hair. "You want a wash and style too, or just a trim?"

"Are you the one who will wash it?" he asked, looking at me in the mirror.

"Yes," I replied.

"Then yeah, wash me up. I'm filthy."

This time I laughed. I doubted Cam had ever been filthy. He was always so clean and put together that he reminded me of a politician.

"Okay. Let's get you clean first, then," I told him, and led him back to the sinks.

I normally didn't think anything of washing men's hair, but the fact that Cam wanted me to wash it made me a little self-conscious. I made sure I had the water at a comfortable temperature for him, then tried really hard to focus on washing his hair and not thinking about the fact that he could probably see down my shirt when I leaned. Most guys closed their eyes when you washed their hair, but Cam's eyes were open.

"You smell really good," he said, making me even more nervous. I didn't like being flirted with when I did hair.

"Thanks," I replied. I quickly finished washing him and got the towel around his head, then led him back to his seat.

When he was back in my chair, his eyes met mine in the mirror. "What are you doing tomorrow night?" he asked.

I was doing nothing. Well, that wasn't true. I was probably watching one of the *Star Wars* movies with my son. "Not sure."

He nodded and looked let down. "Is my not calling going to be held against me?"

No. Not really. I didn't blame him for not calling. I wouldn't have called me either after that craziness.

"No," I assured him as I began combing his hair.

"So if I asked you out for tomorrow night . . . ?"

"I would have to speak with my son first. Then I'd need to talk to his grandparents," I told him.

He nodded. "Fair enough. When you do that, let me know. I'd like another chance. One where we don't run into your son's uncle."

Cam was a nice guy. He was attractive. But he wasn't Dewayne. No one would ever be Dewayne. But I needed the guys I dated to at least make me forget Dewayne. Cam never would. I'd always be missing Dewayne's tattoos and piercings and dreadlocks.

"I think that I'm a waste of your time, Cam. I have baggage, and I'm not emotionally ready to date."

There, I had been honest. Cam frowned, then let out a sigh. "Fair enough. I figured there was more between you and Dewayne Falco than just your son."

I couldn't even argue with him.

I finished cutting his hair, and we talked about the weather, what could possibly be wrong with my car, and the high school cafeteria food. Then he paid me, tipped me way too much, and left.

I might have made a mistake turning him away, but I didn't ever want to hurt someone. I knew how that felt, and there was no point in him wasting his time with me. I was a mess.

Six years ago . . .

DEWAYNE

Preston pulled up outside a house surrounded by cars, with loud music pumping out of the speakers. There were empty beer cans in the yard and even more red Solo cups. A bunch of guys were doing shots off some chick's stomach on the front porch.

"You sure you want to do this? We partied too when we were in school. Ain't like Dustin is doing anything we didn't do," Preston said, looking around at the high school party with illegal drinking going on. Whoever lived here must have been left home alone by really stupid parents.

"This shit ain't Dustin. He has college scouts looking at him. He has a life we can't imagine waiting on him. He shouldn't be here, and he sure as hell shouldn't have Sienna here with him. This isn't safe."

Preston chuckled. "Shit always comes back to Sienna," he said, but I ignored him as we walked up the sidewalk.

A couple of the guys on the basketball team recognized me and called out to me. They were all smashed. I ignored them. They were making a mistake. This wasn't going to get them anywhere but fucking prison.

I wouldn't let that happen to my brother.

"Where's Dustin?" I asked one of them.

"He's got Kimmy up in a bedroom, more than likely," someone called out.

Kimmy? Kimmy the blond cheerleader Kimmy? Oh, fuck no, he wasn't that stupid. She'd slept with Preston our senior year. She'd slept with a lot of my graduating class.

I headed inside and straight up the stairs. Preston was behind me. "He's a kid. We sure as hell weren't relationship material when we were his age. We fucked anything that was hot and had a pussy. You can't blame him for not being satisfied—"

I turned and got in Preston's face, shutting him up. "Don't. Sienna is different. We never had a Sienna. So don't fucking compare that shit. He's fucking up his life."

Preston threw his hands in the air and backed up. "Fine. Go knock some sense into him. Not me. Him. I like my face all nice and pretty."

Preston was hard to get mad at. I turned back around and headed for the first door, opening it and finding some random girl's tits, and her mouth wrapped around a guy's dick.

Next room. I swung open the door just as my brother's name was being screamed by a girl who was not Sienna. Fucking idiot!

"You little dipshit! What the fuck are you doing?" I roared. The girl squealed, and all Dustin did was look back at me and grin. He was drunk. His eyes were bloodshot, and he had a goofy look on his face.

"I'm fucking," he replied, and pumped his hips into the girl, who was scrambling to cover herself. "She's been wanting my dick for two years. I started giving it to her 'cause she likes it hard and dirty."

More information than I needed to know.

"Dude, you so need to shut up before he beats the hell out of you," Preston said from behind me. "Little brother or not, you're drunk and screwing someone who isn't Sienna when you know how he is about Sienna."

"Did you break up with Sienna?" I asked him, trying to figure out why he would be in here with this slut when he had the world in his hands.

"Break up with Sienna? Hell no. She's my girl. Love her. Wouldn't break up with her for this," he said, nodding to the girl underneath him, who cursed at him and slapped his chest.

"You can't love Sienna and do this shit to her," I told him, still trying to figure out what the hell had happened to my brother.

"Yeah, I can. Sienna's my baby. Love her. You just gotta be easy with her. She can't take it hard. Kimmy lets me fuck her in the janitor's closet at school, and she even sucks my dick in the locker room before a game."

Shit. Dustin had lost his mind. "Get dressed. We're leaving. Now."

Dustin stood up. His dick was still hard, and I saw then that he didn't have a condom on. Motherfucker!

"Oh shit, he ain't wrapping that thing up," Preston said, pointing out the obvious.

"You selfish asshole! You're cheating on Sienna and you're not protecting her? What the hell is wrong with you?"

Dustin looked down at his dick and groaned. "Shit. I forgot. I was drinking and she was stroking me outside, and then I was up here and inside her. Forgot about the condom."

"You gotta tell Sienna. She needs to go get checked. Get dressed. I'm taking you home."

Dustin's eyes went wide. "I ain't telling Sienna this shit! She'll break up with me. She won't forgive me, and I need her. She's my girl. Always been my girl. Besides, she's got the best damn titties of any girls I've had."

I took a step toward him, needing to slam my fist into his face, when Preston jumped in front of me and pushed Dustin back. "He's sixteen and he's drunk. Really damn drunk. Calm down. You can make sure Sienna gets tested. Just don't beat the hell out of him while he's like this. He can't fight back."

"No. Can't tell Sienna. Love her. She's my girl. Love her. You can't make her leave me. She's my one and only. You know. You love her too. We both love her. The Falco boys love Sienna Roy. And her pretty titties. Fucking perfect titties."

"Can y'all leave so I can get dressed?" Kimmy asked in an angry screech. "I'm sick of hearing about his love for Sienna and her damn titties. It's me who's pregnant with his baby. Not her. Me. Me who he fucks whenever he needs to get off. Not her. He treats her like a porcelain doll. She's not gonna be his baby momma. I am."

Chapter Seventeen

Present day . . .

SIENNA

Dewayne had actually shown up instead of texting me to take Micah to his parents' on Saturday morning. Then he'd driven me to work, with Micah sitting between us in the truck, excited about going to get breakfast with Dewayne after they dropped me off.

It was easy enough. Micah being there made it easy. I didn't make eye contact with Dewayne if I didn't have to, and I focused on Micah. That was why I was even in this truck with Dewayne: Micah. He did it all for Micah, and I understood that. He'd made sure I understood why he was doing this.

However, when Dewayne came walking into the shop at lunchtime to pick me up, he didn't have Micah with him.

"Where's Micah?" I asked as I picked up my purse.

"My parents have him. We have to go get your car," he replied.

Oh. Well, that was good. I thought. I just hoped I had enough money. I still owed for the towing, too. I wasn't sure who I owed or how much. I would find out once Dewayne and I got in his truck.

"Hey, Dewayne," Gretchen said, and wiggled her long pink fingernails at him, then winked.

He didn't do anything more than nod at her, and then he motioned for the door. "Ready?" he asked.

I waved at Hillary and Gretchen, although at the moment I wasn't in the mood to do anything but scowl at Gretchen. I wished she'd never told me about her and Dewayne. I followed him outside. He opened my door for me, and I climbed inside and buckled up.

Dewayne got in on his side and we were on the road without a word from either of us. I hoped this wasn't going to be a long, awkward ride.

"Reckon you're not gonna be happy with me, but you're gonna have to get over it and understand that I'm doing what's best for Micah."

I tensed up. This didn't sound good.

"I had your car towed to the junkyard where it belonged. It's now scrap metal. Seeing as how I did that, I owe you another car. I'll gladly replace your old one, and although you're ready to punch me in the face right at this moment, you're not going to because I'm driving and because you and I both know Micah needs a safe vehicle. He also needs his momma in a safe vehicle.

What you were driving was as unsafe as it gets. And it was polluting the earth."

I just stared at him. He'd had my car turned into scrap metal. My only means of transportation. My paid-for car was now gone. "I can't believe you did that," I said, still in shock.

"I want you and Micah safe."

We were safe. Well, maybe the car breaking down at night hadn't been safe, but otherwise that car had worked just fine. "I can't just let you buy me a car," I said, my voice raising a notch from the panic. "I can't . . . That isn't something someone else buys you. It's my job to supply a car for me and my son. Not yours."

Dewayne pulled into the Chevrolet car dealership. He was really doing this. I wasn't going to let him. I couldn't.

"I'm buying my nephew a safe vehicle. You can't stop me. I can buy his mother something to safely carry him around in. Someone needs to take care of you, both of you. I'm the uncle. It's my job."

I fisted up my hands and hit my thighs in frustration. "No, it isn't!"

"Yeah, Little Red, it is. Now, I did some research on good family SUVs, and the Tahoe ranked really well. It's safe, and they have one here that's two years old and in great condition. I want you to come see what you think. If you like it, then it's yours. If you don't, then we will go to car lots all damn day until you find something you love."

"You can't afford this," I argued.

He cocked his head to the side. "Yeah, babe, I can. Now get your ass out of my truck and go look at that Tahoe. They're bringing it around now."

Okay. Fine. I would look at it. But he was not buying it for me. For Micah. This was ridiculous.

An hour later I drove my new Chevy Tahoe off the lot and was completely in love. It had everything. Even a sunroof. The radio worked and it had seat warmers. Micah was going to be giddy with excitement over the television that flipped down from the ceiling.

When I had finally given in and admitted to loving the Tahoe, Dewayne had grinned like a little boy on Christmas morning. He had been happy about it. How he was happy about dropping this kind of money on someone made no sense. I was stressing out over the price, but Dewayne assured me that he had the money and could pay cash. That he wanted to do this.

The title would be sent to me with my name on it in a few weeks. I owned this Tahoe. I could drive it for at least the next ten years. The relief made me want to weep. I owned a house and a safe, dependable car now. It made me feel humbled. I had never expected this. Ever.

I glanced in my rearview mirror and watched as Dewayne turned left at the red light, headed to wherever he lived. I had never seen his place. I doubted I ever would unless Micah went there to visit him.

The idea made me sad. I wanted to know what Dewayne's house looked like. I wanted to see his world. His life. But I wasn't ever going to get that privilege. He had made sure I understood that.

I pulled into my driveway, and the front door flew open as Micah came running out with a huge grin on his face. Tabby stood in my doorway, beaming. Dewayne must have called her.

I opened the door, and Micah jumped up in my arms. "Uncle Dewayne bought us this? For real? It's awesome!"

I nodded and blinked away the tears in my eyes. It was awesome.

"It even has a television," I told him, letting him crawl inside to inspect it.

Tabby walked up, wiping her tears and grinning. "He's a good man. He just doesn't realize it. He doubts himself, but my boy is as good as they come. Always has had a heart of gold. Just need him to wake up and see that."

"This is too much. I can't believe he bought this. I'm in awe, and I feel guilty for letting him," I admitted.

She laughed. "Girl, you didn't have a choice. Once Dewayne decides he wants to do something, then you're sunk. He's gonna do it. And he wanted you and Micah to have a safe vehicle. Besides, if he saw how much fun Micah was having checking it out, he might go buy him another one."

She was right. Dewayne was a good man. Much better than

he let himself believe. Was it possible that he needed someone to show him that he was special? Was that it? No woman had ever tried to make him see how wonderful he was inside. Could I?

DEWAYNE

I had finished loading my dishwasher and was headed to the shower when a knock on the door stopped me. I turned and went to open it. Sienna stood there holding a cake box and wore a nervous smile. I was not expecting to see her at my door.

"Hey. Uh, Micah and I made you something. He loved the Tahoe. I had to force him to get out of it. He wanted to stay in it and watch a movie tonight."

That made me smile. We would have to take a road trip in it soon so he could watch his movie. "I'm glad he approves," I said, then stepped back to let her inside.

She looked around, and I could see the surprise on her face that my place was clean. I didn't do well with messy shit. I liked my stuff put away. It was one reason I didn't do roommates. I'd tried that once and almost threw Preston's crap out the window and into the parking lot one day, I'd gotten so sick of it.

"Your mom told Micah you like chocolate. So we made you a chocolate cake. The icing was Micah's job, so it's . . . creative," she said.

I took the box from her hands and nodded toward the kitchen. "Come on," I told her.

I needed to set the cake down and decide how I liked having her in my space. I had imagined her here before, but then, in those fantasies, she was normally naked in my bed or shower. Once she'd even been bent over my couch.

"You're really clean. I don't think I expected that," she said, looking around.

I shrugged. "Don't like things messy. Never have. Well, some things I like to get messy with." I shouldn't have gone there. Not with her here in my place alone. I wanted things, and thinking about doing messy things with her was too damn tempting.

"Oh," she said, blushing, and looked away from me. The pink in her cheeks was one of my favorite things to see. That and her smile. Her eyes twinkled in a way that could make everything else okay.

"When you look at me like that, it makes me forget that you just want to fuck me one time and nothing more." Her words came out of nowhere, and hearing her say "fuck" didn't help me.

"It's hard not to look at you," I admitted. "Always has been."

Sienna let out a nervous laugh. "Well, it's always been hard not to look at you, too. So I guess we both have a problem. If we slept together, I'd want more of it. Once would never be enough. One kiss wasn't enough. I don't think I could ever get my fill."

What the hell . . . ?

Sienna was just laying it out there. Why? I'd told her that I couldn't be what she wanted. I had tried to hold her at arm's length, so why would she walk into my apartment and tell me she could never get enough of me? That was brave. Unbelievably so. It was time I admitted the truth too.

"If I get a taste of what it feels like to be inside you, I won't be able to stop. Ever. I've been addicted to you since I was seventeen years old. I fought it because you were my brother's. Then I fought it because I wasn't worthy of you. It's my fault he wrapped his car around that tree that night. I'd threatened him, and he was drunk and ran off."

I couldn't tell her the rest. That I had been mad that he had gotten Kimmy pregnant and had been cheating on Sienna for over a year. I never wanted her to know that. Ever.

"Dustin made his own mistakes," she replied. "He chose to drink and party, and he chose to drive his car when he shouldn't have. I begged him not to drink, but he always laughed it off, saying he was only having fun and wasn't hurting anyone. I let myself believe him. But in the end Dustin made the reckless decision that took his life. He missed out on knowing our son. He missed out on his future as a star. He missed out on so much. But it was no one's fault but his. I blamed myself for so long, but I know now that he made that decision. Not me. And not you."

No one had ever told me that. I knew it was true, but no one had ever said those words to me. Still, I knew what I'd said to Dustin to send him racing back to Sienna in a panic. He was worried I was going to tell her what he was doing. He wanted to stop me. I'd never imagined he would get behind the wheel.

"I loved him. I miss him every damn day," I said, gripping the edge of the countertop. I never talked about Dustin like this. It hurt too much.

"I loved him too. He was my best friend. He gave me the greatest gift on earth before he left me. I have Micah."

I wanted her memories of Dustin to remain intact. I owed my brother that much. Because I wasn't staying away from her anymore. She was right—Dustin had made his own decisions, and he hadn't cherished what he had. I would. I'd been cherishing her from afar for so damn long.

"Stay. Eat some cake with me," I said, not wanting her to leave. "Where's Micah?"

"Your parents'," she replied.

"Can you stay the night?"

Her eyes went wide, and she took a deep breath. "Are you sure?"

"Yes."

Then she nodded. "Yes."

I shoved away from the counter. "Sienna."

"Yes," she replied a little breathlessly as I closed the space between us.

"Can we eat the cake later? Much later? Like for breakfast?"

She nodded again just before my mouth captured hers.

Chapter Eighteen

SIENNA

He was everywhere all at once. My head was spinning, and if he hadn't backed me up against the wall, I would have crumpled to the ground. It was overwhelming and thrilling.

Dewayne sucked on my bottom lip before trailing kisses across my jaw, then settled in to torture the spot behind my ear. "Wanted to do this for so long," he whispered against my skin. "This one spot. All over. Fuck, Sienna, I don't know if I can go slow. I want to so much, but right now I just wanna be inside you."

I wanted Dewayne any way I could have him. Knowing that he wanted more with me than one night and that he wanted this made me willing to grant his every wish. "We have all night," I told him.

Then I was off the ground, and I wrapped my legs around his waist as he walked me through a door off to the side of the kitchen and straight to a king-size bed in the middle of the room. "Naked and on my bed. Fucking want that. Now," he said, jerking his shirt off and tossing it away. He reached for my shirt, and I raised my hands willingly and let him pull it off me. His eyes looked like they had caught fire when he took in the sight of me in my bra.

"Take it off. I want to watch," he said, not looking away from my chest.

I unhooked the back clasp and let my bra fall forward. Then I pulled it off my arms and moved it aside. I didn't care where it ended up. I just cared about the look of hunger on Dewayne's face, and knowing it was me he was looking at like that.

It sounded like he muttered something like "magic tits," but I wasn't sure I'd heard him right. His hands were on the waistband of my shorts, tugging them down, so all thoughts of his muttering left me. I had been completely naked with only one person, and he had been a boy. He had also never taken his time with me like this. Or looked at me like he was in awe.

Dewayne knelt down in front of me and pushed my knees apart. I sucked in a breath as he kissed my knee and looked up at me through hooded eyes. "I love these red curls. So fucking hot."

Oh my.

"Lay back, Sienna. And keep these legs open for me," he

said as he stood up and unzipped his jeans. I wanted to watch him shove those jeans down, but I did as he asked, trying hard to see him. I had fantasized about all of him for a long time too.

"I'm gonna have to taste you first. I want inside you, baby, but I gotta kiss this," he said as his hand cupped me between the legs. I was exposed, and I should have felt vulnerable. But it was Dewayne. It felt right. It was exciting.

Dewayne lowered himself to his knees and picked up my right foot, then kissed it before putting my leg over his shoulder. Then he did the same with the left. The warmth of his breath was so close I shivered.

"Smell like a fucking candy store," he said just before his tongue slid against me. The sensation was amazing. I cried out and reached for something. I ended up with handfuls of the blanket underneath me.

With each stroke of his tongue my body bucked, and tremors of pleasure coursed through me.

"Dewayne," I whimpered as the intensity got to be too much. I was so close to something I'd only had with myself, alone in my room.

"You close?" he asked, lifting his head. His tongue came out to lick his lips, and nothing in my life had ever been as sexy as that man.

"Yes," I replied, breathless.

He bent his head, then pressed a kiss to the sensitive spot

that always needed the most attention, and I moaned, unable to keep quiet. This was all more than I had ever expected.

Then he stood up, and the solid, muscled body covered in colorful tattoos was there on display. I was so close to an orgasm that just seeing him like this almost sent me over the edge. Every hard line of his body was beautiful. I wanted to touch him everywhere. Then my eyes dropped and went wide with sudden panic. I wasn't an expert on penis size since I had only been with a sixteen-year-old boy, but that was big. Maybe too big. Sex had always been uncomfortable with Dustin, and sometimes hurt. He said it was because he was too big and I was too tight, but that . . . Oh no.

"Much as I like you looking, I'm not feeling very patient right now," he said before lowering himself over me. "God, you're perfect," he said, then kissed the tip of one of my breasts.

He wasn't going to think I was perfect when he didn't fit inside me. Or when I was screaming in pain and begging him to stop. This was what I had wanted for so long, and now I was positive it wasn't going to happen. I tensed and closed my eyes, praying that I didn't embarrass myself and do something like cry. If I could just suffer through the pain . . . I would do anything for Dewayne. I just hoped I could do it quietly.

"Sienna?" Dewayne's voice was concerned. Of course it was. I was acting like an idiot and he hadn't even tried to get inside me yet.

I opened my eyes and looked up at him. I was so sorry. I

wanted this. I wanted him. But the pain. It had been bad at first with Dustin, and I knew once a guy got going he couldn't stop just because you were crying in pain. He had to finish.

"What's wrong, baby?" he said as he brushed my hair out of my face with his thumb, then ran it over my bottom lip. He was so sweet. Who would have thought Dewayne Falco could be this sweet?

"It always hurt . . . before. Always. And you're bigger . . ." God, I hated this. Reminding him I'd slept with his younger brother was a mood killer.

He frowned. "It should have only hurt a little bit the first time."

I had to explain this. As humiliating as it was, I had to tell him. "I'm, uh . . . It always hurt. I never enjoyed it." There. I admitted it.

Dewayne closed his eyes and let out a hissing sound through his teeth. When he opened them, he locked his gaze with mine. "This won't hurt. I swear to you, Sienna, it'll feel good, baby. I'll make sure you see stars."

I almost believed him. With that fierce look in his eyes, it was easy to believe. But the fact remained that he was much bigger than Dustin had been. "But I haven't had sex in a long time. I was tight then." I had also had a kid, but that was five years ago, so any stretching that created was more than likely all gone now.

Dewayne lowered his head until his lips brushed my ear.

"You're tight now. But you're also so fucking wet and ready," he said in a whisper, just as his finger stroked the tender heat between my legs.

I gasped and Dewayne chuckled. "That's it, baby. Let me take care of you. I'm not ever gonna hurt you again. In any way. I swear it."

Even if it did hurt, I would take it. This was Dewayne. I wanted Dewayne. Deep down I had always wanted Dewayne.

He leaned up, and I watched him reach for a small square foil wrapper, which he tore open with his teeth. Then he rolled the condom down. If I wasn't so scared of sex, I could appreciate watching him do this more.

Then he was over me again, and his lips found mine. The gentle glide of his tongue as he took what he wanted eased my fear just before I felt his tip nudge my entrance. "Easy, baby. I'm gonna be gentle. But you need to relax," he said in a husky, strained voice as he tucked his head into the curve of my neck.

Slowly he eased inside me. With each inch that filled me there was no pain, only pleasure. Maybe I wasn't as tight any-more. I hoped so.

"You okay?" he asked me, holding himself up over me. I smiled in relief and nodded.

Our gazes locked as he eased in more and I lifted my hips to take him. The stretching felt good and the fullness was incredible. But more than that . . . this was right. I knew it now. What had been wrong all those years ago—it hadn't been Dustin who had claimed my heart. I just loved him like you would a friend. He was what I knew.

Dewayne, however, made me feel things no one ever had before. I had been too young to realize it then, but now it was all very clear. This was the Falco boy I was always meant to be with.

"Sienna, you gotta stop lifting that sweet ass, baby. This is the fucking tightest pussy in the world, and all I want to do is move hard and fast. But I'm taking it slow. Help me take it slow."

He wanted to move but he wasn't. He was being gentle for me. I didn't know men could go slowly. With that realization, Dewayne took another little piece of my heart. I wanted to protect myself from getting hurt, but I trusted him. I trusted him more than I'd ever trusted anyone. Besides, I wasn't sure he hadn't taken my heart years ago and not given it back. There wasn't much left for me to protect anymore.

"It feels good. It doesn't hurt at all. I want you," I assured him.

With that bit of encouragement, he sank into me completely and let out a groan of pleasure. "God, woman, you're squeezing the hell out of me."

Feeling braver, I wrapped my legs around him and arched into him.

With his body that was meant to be appreciated for the sculpted perfection that it was, Dewayne held himself over me as he began rocking in and out of me. I wrapped my hands around his bulging biceps and held on. Each time he sank into me fully, he touched something that sent sparks of such intense shocks through my body that I wanted to beg him to go faster. I wanted that feeling.

There was moaning and begging that I was positive was coming from me. After the fourth time he brushed that special spot deep inside me, I became so delirious with need that I no longer knew what I was saying. I just never wanted it to stop.

The explosion of sensation that went off in my body shocked me. All I could do was hold on to Dewayne as I cried out his name. Trusting him not to let me go, I fell into the uncharted bliss without fear.

Somewhere far away I heard Dewayne shout, and his body tensed over mine. I wrapped myself tighter around him as he eased down on top of me. The ability to move had been taken from me already. A lazy, smooth heaven enveloped me, and I wanted to share it with Dewayne in my arms.

"Magic fucking pussy," he whispered as his forehead dropped to my collarbone. His breathing was hard as he gasped and shuddered. "Fuck," he said, then pressed a kiss to my shoulder.

A giggle built inside me, and I didn't even try to hold back. I was happy. So very happy.

Dewayne lifted his head and grinned at me. "Why you laughing, Little Red?"

I pressed my lips together to control the giggles. "You called my, uh . . . you know . . . magic."

A smirk touched his mouth, and I wanted nothing more than to kiss those full red lips. "It is magic. Which means you're stuck with me. Never thought I'd find magic pussy. Never wanted it, but damn, I do now. I intend to keep you."

I wanted to be kept, but I had only really wanted that with Dewayne.

I touched his lips with my fingers, and he pulled one of my fingers into his mouth and sucked. The fire inside me began to stir again as I watched his mouth on my skin. He let it pop free. "I need to make sure you're okay. Check you out personally and see if everything feels good and I didn't hurt you. Then I can make you messy again."

He hadn't hurt me, but I liked the idea of him checking to make sure, and I wanted to get messy again. "Do I have to get cleaned up first?" I wanted messy again now.

Dewayne chuckled. "Needy, magic pussy. Fuck me, I got lucky. But yeah, I have to take care of what's mine first. Then I'll clean you up real good. But don't worry. I intend to make you scream my name at least once, maybe twice, in the shower."

My eyes widened and I squirmed underneath him. I'd never taken a shower with anyone. The idea of it excited me. "Okay. Let's go get clean."

DEWAYNE

I leaned against the bedroom door frame, holding a plate of chocolate cake while watching Sienna curled up asleep in the middle of my bed. She looked so small there all alone. I didn't intend to leave her there long, but I knew she needed more sleep. I'd woken her up three times last night, unable to keep my hands off her.

My need to keep her safe and protected had just found an all-new level of possessiveness. Sienna wasn't just Micah's mother, she was my woman. Mine. I didn't want her sleeping without me. I didn't want her waking up without me. I didn't fucking want her bathing without me.

There was a good fucking chance I was completely obsessed with her. I didn't get obsessed with anything. Ever. But Sienna was different. She'd always been different. She'd found something inside me and brought it to life when we were kids. After years of fighting it and forgetting her, I had given in and let myself feel. And I fucking felt a lot. More than I thought possible.

The look my daddy gave my momma when she walked into a room now made complete sense to me. When Preston kept Amanda latched at his side like he couldn't breathe without her, and Cage growled at any man he thought looked at Eva too long, I got that. So fucking completely got that.

Even Krit and his inability to sing onstage without having Blythe near him—that made sense to me. Hell, I was pretty damn sure I was going to become so much worse than any of them.

"You gonna eat all that by yourself?" Sienna asked, and I looked up from her long, silky legs to see her eyes halfway open as she looked at me.

"I'm gonna feed the sexy woman in my bed," I told her. I shoved off from my stance against the door frame and walked over to the bed to sit down beside her.

She moved to sit up and the sheet fell, letting the most amazing set of tits in the world free. Fuck yeah. Those were mine.

"They aren't hungry. I am," Sienna teased as she pulled the sheet back up to cover herself.

I jerked my gaze off her chest and rested it on her face. The sleepy, well-taken-care-of smile on her lips and her hooded eyes made it hard to think about feeding her. I wanted to be in her. Again.

"Open up," I told her, and took a forkful of cake and slipped it into her pretty pink mouth.

"I was thinking while you slept that it would be fun to rub this icing on several parts of your body and lick it off. Think we might have to try that later."

Sienna ducked her head, but I saw the smile on her face. She scooted closer to me until her front pressed against my arm. When she looked back up at me, there was a mischievous twinkle in her eyes. "Only if I can put some on you and lick it off."

"Anytime you want to lick me, baby, you say the word and I'm yours. I don't care where we are. If there's a chance I can have that mouth on me, then I'll want it. I'll always want it."

She dropped her gaze to my lap, and my already semi-erect cock went full-blown. I reached over and cupped her face with my hand and tilted it so that her eyes were on mine. "This thing with you and me. It's real. You got me. Just us. No one else. Not letting you go, Sienna. I've waited too damn long, and now that I finally have you, I sure as hell ain't leaving you."

She didn't respond at first, but I could see the questions in her eyes. She'd come over here to bring me a cake and tell me how she felt about me. Then I'd taken it from that to an exclusive relationship overnight. Literally.

"You said you don't do this," she said, almost in a whisper.

"I don't. Never have. Never wanted to. But then, I'd never had you. I always thought I'd never find this. I wasn't looking for it. But now that I've got it, I won't let it go. I'll do whatever I have to in order to keep you happy."

Her big eyes filled with tears and she blinked, wetting those long eyelashes of hers. "Then we're an us," she said with a sweet smile that made my heart do funny shit.

"I'm warning you now that I'm not gonna be easy to deal with. I want you by my side. In my bed. I don't want you away from me. I don't want to do that space shit. I'm gonna be in your space every fucking chance I get."

Sienna laughed and reached over to dip her finger in the icing. "Hmm . . . Dewayne Falco doesn't want to be apart from me. He wants to be in my space. I guess there could be worse things in life than that," she said in a serious tone. "If you're in my space, then I'll get more chances to do things like this." She held up her finger and grinned. "Pull down those sweats," she ordered.

I did as instructed and gripped the sheets beside me as Sienna coated the head of my dick with the icing on her finger. My breathing was getting faster as she took her time. My patience was just about to snap when she lowered her head and her tongue darted out and licked the tip in a teasing stroke.

"Mmmm," she moaned.

I wanted to let her have her fun, but I was so close to begging it wasn't funny. After three more licks her mouth opened and slid down over me. The roar of triumph that tore out of me only encouraged her more. She sucked and began sliding her mouth up and down my length.

I moved her hair back so I could watch her mouth take me deep. "So fucking gorgeous," I said as she looked up at me.

I knew in that moment that if this woman asked me to walk on water, I'd find a fucking way.

Chapter Nineteen

SIENNA

Dewayne had agreed to stay over at his parents' while I talked to Micah this morning. He had wanted to be there with me, but for five years it had been just me and Micah. No one else got my attention. Just him. I didn't doubt he'd love having Dewayne in our lives more than he already was, but I also wanted to make sure he felt secure in where he stood.

Micah had talked about his night the whole walk over from the Falcos' to our house. Apparently, Dave had watched not one but two of the *Star Wars* movies with Micah. And they'd eaten popcorn and cookies. Mama T had said she might get a swimming pool in the backyard when Micah told her he liked to swim. She and Dave were going to look into it. Those two were going to spoil my kid, and I loved it.

The five-year-old didn't notice the goofy smile on my face. But I knew it was there. I couldn't stop thinking about last night and this morning. Dewayne had been everything I'd dreamed about and more. I was ready to give him everything.

"Uncle Dewayne said he would see me in a little bit. Is he coming to play with me today?" Micah asked hopefully. That was a good thing. Micah wanted his uncle around. Dewayne wouldn't be someone Micah might worry would take me away from him. He fit perfectly into our lives.

"Yes. If he said he's coming over, then he will be here. You can trust Uncle Dewayne to do what he says he'll do. He loves you."

Micah beamed. He liked feeling loved. He'd always had my love, but this extra love was something he soaked up.

"Actually, I wanted to talk to you about Uncle Dewayne before he comes over here," I told him as we walked into the house.

"About what?"

I led him over to the sofa and pulled him into my lap. "You're my number one. You know that, right?"

Micah nodded.

"And you love your uncle Dewayne as much as he loves you."

Micah nodded again.

"Well, I love your uncle Dewayne too." *I did?* I loved him. I did. Oh wow. I *did*.

Micah smiled. "Because he's family."

Uh-oh. I'd forgotten about that conversation. I had to

explain this. "Well, actually, Uncle Dewayne is your dad's family. Not exactly mine. But he's yours, so I called him mine, too."

Micah scrunched up his nose. "So we don't have the same family?"

This is what I get for lying to the kid. I wasn't ever doing that again. Lesson learned.

"No, we do. . . . It's just that you're actually related to Uncle Dewayne. I'm not. He is your daddy's brother, but he's not related to me. I wasn't married to your daddy. We never got a chance to do that. Remember? I explained that to you."

Micah nodded, but his nose was still scrunched up. "Okay, so can Uncle Dewayne take you on dates, then?"

Sighing in relief, I nodded. "Yes. He can. And he wants to, but we want it to be okay with you."

Micah grinned and made a whooping sound.

"I take that as a yes."

He nodded vigorously. "Can he sleep over in my room?"

Oh my.

"Well, he will be here more often. He wants to spend more time with us. But if he sleeps over, your bed isn't big enough for him. He's a big guy."

Micah's expression got really serious. "We need to get him a big bed so he can sleep over."

Okay, this was getting way off track. Right now we needed

to focus on the topic of Dewayne being around more often. Not having sleepovers.

Micah jumped down, walked over to the door, and looked out. "When is he coming over?"

"As soon as I text him and tell him you're ready for him."

Micah turned and ran toward his room. "Text him. I'm getting my football."

That was way too easy.

I pulled my phone out of my pocket and quickly sent Dewayne a text that Micah and his football were waiting on him.

I hadn't even set my phone down when the front door of the Falcos' opened up and Dewayne stepped out. He must have been waiting anxiously for that text. He was so big and tough, but the little boy inside him that he never let others see owned me.

"Looks like he's on his way over," I called to Micah.

Micah came running around the corner with his football tucked under his arm. "We're gonna play some ball," he told me before letting the screen door slam behind him.

I walked over to the door and watched as Micah ran straight for Dewayne and held up the football. The smile on Dewayne's face as he looked at my son made right everything that had been wrong.

His eyes lifted from Micah and found me, and then he winked before looking back at Micah.

I stood there and watched them toss the ball back and forth. Dewayne showed Micah how to improve his throw, and I watched as Micah worked hard to get it right. I finally let myself accept something I'd been fighting since I was fourteen years old. I had always loved Dewayne. It had always been him. Dustin had been my best friend and I'd been his. But my heart . . . Dewayne had stolen that in front of a locker on my first day of high school.

Chapter Twenty

SIENNA

They hadn't let me out of my bedroom since my doctor's visit. I had been throwing up so bad for two mornings in a row that my mother had taken me to the doctor. She'd thought I had a stomach virus.

But we had both been surprised when the doctor informed us that I was pregnant. Not sick. *Pregnant.*

Mother hadn't spoken to me the whole way home, and then she'd sent me to my room and ordered me to stay. My dad never once came to see me. Mother showed up with food at my door three times a day. I even had to open the door and ask to go to the bathroom.

I knew they were upset. I was terrified. Dustin was gone, and I had no one I could tell. No one to share this with, and now my parents were shutting me out. That scared me more than anything. The one thing I could be sure of was that this baby was safe. My father was too religious to make me have an abortion. For once I was thankful for his strict beliefs.

But I had questions, and I had no one to ask. My mother refused to speak to me when she brought me my meals. I didn't have a phone in my room, and no one had stopped by to see me. That wasn't too surprising. Dustin's friends had accepted me, but they had never really been my friends.

So I sat here in my window seat and watched the world outside. I watched the people who came and visited the Falcos. People were still bringing them food. It was what we did here in the South. If someone died, you took their family food. I never understood that. I hadn't been able to eat for days after Dustin's death. I had cried and slept. That had been all I could manage.

At his funeral, what little strength I had to keep it together was gone the second I saw Dewayne Falco's shoulders slumped, jerking harshly from crying. I never even imagined that Dewayne could cry. He was so tough and larger than life. But in that moment, seeing him broken, I lost it all over again. I hated seeing him in so much pain. He loved his brother, and Dustin had worshipped Dewayne.

At night whenever I closed my eyes, the image of Dewayne sobbing over his brother's grave haunted me. I had wanted to hold him even though I knew he wouldn't welcome it. No one could console him. No one could bring back Dustin.

We had all lost him.

Including the little life inside me.

I touched my stomach reverently, closed my eyes, and dreamed of the child inside. What would he or she look like? I wondered if it would have its father's smile and charm. If it would grow up a Falco or a Roy. If the Falcos would accept this baby. I knew my parents were upset, but surely Tabby would love him.

I opened my eyes just as Dewayne walked across the street toward my house. Quickly I moved back behind the curtains and watched as he stepped up onto my porch. The doorbell rang, and I hurried over to my bedroom door to crack it open so I could hear him. Why was he here? I hadn't seen him leave his parents' house much over the past few weeks.

"Hello, Dewayne," my mother said in a gentler tone than I'd expected. At least she respected the fact that he'd lost his brother. She didn't have to be angry at him because I was pregnant. I was just glad my dad was at work.

"Is Sienna here?" he asked.

He was here to see me. Someone to talk to. Someone else who was hurting and lost without Dustin. Someone I trusted above anyone else.

"No. She isn't here any longer. She's been sent to a . . . facility up North. She had issues dealing with everything, and she wasn't right emotionally."

What?

"Oh. Uh, I didn't realize she'd left. I . . . When is she coming back?"

"I don't know. Not anytime soon," my mother replied.

What? Was she serious? I was right here in my bedroom like I had been for a week now. Did she honestly plan to keep me locked up like this? Wasn't that illegal? I had to see a doctor at some point.

"Is there a number where I can reach her?"

"No. She can't communicate with anyone here. It upsets her. Talking to you will upset her. She needs time and medication."

Holy crap! My mother was making me out to be a crazy person.

"Well, when she's ready to talk to someone again, can you please have her call me? I can leave my number. I'd like to check on her. See if she's doing well. I don't want her to think we don't care. We know she lost him too."

I got a funny tightening in my chest that only Dewayne Falco managed to inspire. How could someone like Dewayne, with his party-boy ways, be so incredibly sweet? He'd been like that my freshman year. He always seemed to be there when I needed him.

"Sure. I'll give her your number," Mother said in a clipped voice. I'd never see Dewayne's number. She'd burn it first.

"Thanks. Tell her that I came by and that I'm thinking about her."

"Okay. Thank you, Dewayne. Tell your parents they are in our prayers. You all are."

"Yes, ma'am," he said.

I closed my door quietly, then ran back over to my window and watched as Dewayne walked away. I would find a way to see him and talk to him. He'd made the first move, and now it was my turn to make a move. He would love this baby. It was part of Dustin. If my parents wanted to lock me up, he could help me escape. He was older. He would know what to do. I just had to find a way to get to him.

The next morning before the sun came up, my mother woke me and hurried me out to my father's station wagon, then handed me a suitcase before she climbed into the passenger seat. My father was already in the driver's seat. I looked over at him, but he didn't say a word. He didn't even turn to look at me.

"Where are we going?" I asked, almost afraid she was about to make good on that story she'd told Dewayne. I wasn't crazy. Surely they couldn't get doctors to keep me if I was perfectly sane.

"Your aunt Cathy's. She's agreed to take you in until you've had the baby."

That was the last thing my mother said to me. We rode in

silence the eleven hours it took to drive to Fort Worth, Texas. My father never once acknowledged my existence. When we arrived, they unloaded me and handed me my suitcase. Spoke in whispered voices with my aunt Cathy, who I had never met before, then drove away without a good-bye.

Present day . . .

DEWAYNE

Micah lay sprawled out over me, fast asleep while Darth Vader kicked ass and took names on the television. The original plan had been to watch *Pirates of the Caribbean*. But then Micah said his mother liked Captain Jack and that we had to wait on her to start the movie.

Hell no, Sienna wasn't going to sit here and look at Johnny Fucking Depp. I had ejected that DVD really damn fast and stuck in one of the *Star Wars* discs. I didn't even care which one it was. Just so Sienna wasn't thinking about some other man.

Sienna walked into the room with that silky little wrap around her and her hair in damp curls, her face scrubbed free of makeup. "Is he asleep?" she asked, moving toward us.

"Yeah," I said, wondering if she had anything on under that wrap.

"Let's get him into bed," she said, bending down to scoop him up.

HOLD ON TIGHT

"I got him," I told her.

"Okay." She stepped back and let me stand up with him, and then she led the way to his room and pulled his covers back so I could tuck him in. Tonight we'd made sure he was bathed and in his pajamas before movie time.

She bent down and kissed his little cheek.

"Love you, Momma," he muttered with his eyes closed.

"Love you more," she replied.

When she turned to leave the room, I bent down and ruffled his hair. He was such a little thing. So much like his daddy at that age.

"Love you, Uncle Dewayne," he said in that same little groggy voice.

My throat closed up, and I had to swallow hard to loosen it up before I could speak. "Love you, kiddo," I told him.

He pulled the covers under his chin and snuggled deeper into his bed.

This moment was all because of Sienna. She'd made this possible.

I fucking loved her. Not just because she'd given me this kid to help heal what I'd lost, but because she'd stolen a piece of my soul with those big eyes and that sweet smile when she was fourteen. I'd wanted to be close to her and keep her safe. I hadn't exactly known why then, I'd just known I wanted her happy. It was important to me.

But I knew why now. She was special. The kind of special that is hard to find in this life. The kind of special most people don't get to touch. It's the rare kind that, when you find it, you know it's worth fighting for.

Her hand softly touched my arm. "Today went well." Her voice was a whisper.

I wrapped my fingers around her small hand and walked out of the room with her by my side.

When she closed the door behind her, I was able to peek down the front of her wrap to see that she was in fact naked under there. Hell yeah.

"I hope he's a deep sleeper, because I got some plans that involve you naked with those long legs of yours over my shoulders."

Sienna glanced back up at me with wide eyes. "Tonight?"

"Fuck yeah, tonight. I hope you don't think I'm going home without you. I told you I wasn't going anywhere and, baby, I was speaking real literal. If you're here, then I'm here."

"Oh," she said as she swayed toward me slightly.

"Yeah, *oh*. Get your ass in that room and let me unwrap my present," I said, turning her toward her bedroom door and walking her inside, then locking it behind me.

The double bed that sat in the middle of the room was so damn small. Sleeping on that was going to be tough, but I'd have my king-size one moved in tomorrow. Tonight we could deal with a double.

"Dewayne?"

I tore my eyes off the small bed and my plans and focused on the almost-naked beauty in front of me. "Yeah?"

She fidgeted with the satin belt, keeping me from seeing all her creamy pale skin underneath. "You staying here is moving fast. I don't want Micah to get his hopes up if in a couple of weeks you realize this isn't what you want."

She didn't get it. Of course she didn't. Sienna Roy didn't understand that she was my one. I had a lifetime to show her just how perfect she was for me.

"This ain't something I'm trying out, Sienna. I don't fucking try shit out. I either want it or I don't. And I've wanted you since I was seventeen years old. Admitting that shit ain't easy. It felt wrong for so long because I love Dustin. I'll always love him, and I'll miss him to the day I die. But he had what I desired, and more than anything I wanted you to be happy. I thought Dustin was who would make you smile. He was who you loved. So I made sure you got what you wanted. But he didn't see what he had. He wasn't careful with it. He didn't cherish it, and in the end he lost it all too young. So I won't be changing my mind in a few weeks. I don't do this shit. I never did this shit. Because they were never you."

Sienna inhaled deeply as she stared at me. I waited on her to say something, anything, to assure me that I wasn't alone here. That she felt something more. That this was different for her.

She reached for the belt on her wrap and tugged it open, letting it fall and giving me the view I'd been wanting. "Show me," she said softly.

Confused, I looked up from her tits to her eyes. "Show you?"

She nodded. "Show me with your body just how different this is for you."

Oh, fuck yes. I could do that.

"Challenge accepted," I said, closing the space between us and shoving the wrap off her arms and letting it fall to the floor in a heap.

She shivered as I ran a finger from the valley between her breasts to her navel, then back up again. So soft. So perfect. "Mine," I told her.

Her breathing hitched, and it made her tits jiggle. Fuck, that was nice.

Chapter Twenty-One

SIENNA

When I pulled into the driveway, my father's station wagon sat in the driveway right behind Dewayne's truck. I'd only been at work four hours, and Dewayne hadn't called me to let me know my mother was here. Because that was the only person it could be. I hadn't seen her in six years, and those last memories weren't happy ones.

And she was in that house with my baby. I didn't even grab my purse before I bolted out of the car and took off running. When I reached the door, it was locked. The keys were in my hands. I'd at least pulled them out of the ignition in my hurry. Unlocking the door, I ran inside.

"Micah?" I called out. "Dewayne?"

No answer. I couldn't call her name. What did I even call her? Mom? She hadn't been that when I needed it most. I walked through the house, but it was empty. No one was here. Could they be at the Falcos'?

The front door opened, and I hurried back to the living room. But the sight of her made me stop. Her hair was gray now. Completely gray. I had been born to my parents late in life and my mother's hair had already started to gray when I lived at home. Seeing it completely gray now was startling. Her face looked like it had aged ten years instead of six, and she was thinner.

"Sienna," she said with an uneasy smile. "You look beautiful."

I looked different too. She'd sent off a sixteen-year-old girl. I was a woman now. A woman with a child.

"Where are Micah and Dewayne?" I asked.

She looked hurt, but she covered it up quickly. I would not feel guilty for that. She had abandoned me. I could never hurt her as badly as she had hurt me. Nothing compared.

"I don't know. I knocked and no one answered, so I walked around back, then heard a car drive up. I didn't recognize the fancy car, but it seems you're doing well now, from the looks of it."

That meant Dewayne and Micah were at the Falcos', and the moment Dewayne looked outside and saw my father's car in the drive, he'd be over here fast. I wanted him here. I just wanted Micah to stay there. She'd given us this house and given Micah that room, but seeing her now and remembering, I wasn't ready to forgive her.

"You never called. I had hoped you would call," she said.

"I know what that feels like. I had hoped you would call once too. Or at least give a shit."

She flinched. Again, I would not feel guilty. She did this to us. To me. "The Falcos know about Micah now, I take it? Since Dewayne is with him."

"Yeah. They missed five years of his life because letters I sent never made it to them. Aunt Cathy says I need to talk to you about that."

Mother looked as if that didn't surprise her. She must have gotten a call from her sister about it.

The door behind her opened, and Dewayne filled the space. A fierce, protective glare was on his face, and his body was tensed and ready to defend me. He stepped around my mother and stood in front of me just slightly. "You okay?" he asked, his gaze softening for me.

I nodded, then reached for his hand. His large one engulfed mine.

"I should have figured this would happen. I knew when you came to see her the day before we took her to Texas that it was more than just checking on her." Mother's voice wasn't condemning or judgmental. More like relieved.

"You told me she was already gone," Dewayne said, turning to look back at my mother.

Mother at least looked apologetic. "I had a pregnant sixteen-year-old daughter, and the father of her child was dead. I didn't know what to do. I was trying to save her future. She was too young to make the right decisions."

The right decisions? Hauling me off and trying to force me to give up my baby was not the right decision.

"Keeping Micah was the best decision of my life," I yelled, unable to control the anger burning inside me at the idea of her not wanting my son.

She nodded. "Yes, it was. You knew better than we did. You knew you could be a good mother. A better mother than I was to you. You showed us all that you would fight to give him a life. And you've done a wonderful job. I'm proud of you. I didn't make you the woman you are, but I'm still proud of you."

My eyes stung with unshed tears, and I gulped down air to keep from sobbing. "You have no idea what it was like. Loving him all on my own. Trying to be enough for him. Trying to be mother and father to him. Telling him how special he was and that he was my world while he asked questions about not having the family other kids had. You don't know! You don't know what it was like! He needed you. I needed you." The sobs stopped me from saying any more. Then Dewayne's arms were around me, holding me.

I had imagined this moment a million times since the day she drove out of my life. Never had it been like this. Never had I broken down like this. I was always resolute and strong. I was always proud of myself and would show her I hadn't needed them. I hadn't needed her. But never did I break down and cry.

The lost girl who didn't know how she was going to do it alone was back. She hadn't been gone. Not really. All along she'd been there underneath the surface. That girl was a fighter, but she was also hiding so much pain. So much betrayal.

"Your father . . . he was devastated. We had tried so hard to protect you. To keep you safe and away from bad decisions. We trusted Dustin. We trusted you. But then Dustin was gone, and you were pregnant. We couldn't see another way."

I wiped at my eyes, and Dewayne soothed me with slow strokes down my head and back. I had to pull it together. I had to get through this. I was strong. I had grown up fast, and for a moment I needed to be that girl again. I needed to tell her what she had done to me. And tell her what I had done for myself.

I moved, and Dewayne eased his hold on me but kept his hand on my back, letting me know he was there. He wasn't leaving me, and I wasn't alone. He would have been there back then, too, if he'd only been given the chance. How different Micah's life would have been.

My mother and father had taken so much from him. I didn't know if I was capable of forgiving that. Hurting me was one thing, but hurting Micah was another.

"Micah deserved to know the Falcos. He was robbed of that. They were robbed of that for five years. What did you do with the letters, Mother? Where did they go if they didn't go to the Falcos? I wrote dozens. I sent photos. For years I tried to reach them. And all along my letters never got there."

Mother sighed wearily and crossed her arms over her chest in a defensive posture. Then she looked up at Dewayne. "I didn't want them to use you and your baby. They had lost Dustin, and then they'd suffered the blow of that Bart girl aborting Dustin's baby. I didn't want the world to know you were pregnant with his son too. If they knew, then everyone else would know. You'd not only be a teen mom, but you'd be one of Dustin Falco's many. I couldn't let that happen to you. You deserved more."

I heard what she was saying, but . . . it wasn't sinking in. It didn't make sense.

"Kimmy?" I asked, trying to understand why she thought Kimmy Bart had aborted Dustin's baby.

My mother's eyes flared with something I didn't understand as she looked at Dewayne. "You didn't tell her," my mother accused.

Dewayne didn't speak.

He wasn't talking, and my mother was angry. She was angry at Dewayne.

About Kimmy Bart. And a baby.

"Kimmy was pregnant too?" I asked, still trying to process this.

My mother's eyes softened with sympathy and something close to sorrow. "I'm sorry, Sienna. I thought by now you would have heard. I didn't know they'd kept that from you. You're old enough and it's been long enough that you can handle the truth. Dustin Falco wasn't sleeping with just you. Kimmy Bart was pregnant with his baby too. Except she was further along than you, and Dustin knew about it when he died. Kimmy made sure everyone in town knew he was hiding it from you."

Something inside me died too at that moment. Something I would never get back.

DEWAYNE

Sienna shut down right in front of my eyes. All emotion left her face, and she just stared straight ahead. The one thing I never wanted her to know, her fucking useless excuse for a mother just tells her without warning or preparation. I'd tried to stop her, but the horror of Sienna knowing robbed me of words. I'd been frozen in this awful reality.

"Baby, look at me," I said, reaching for her, but she stepped back. She didn't look at me, and instead she moved away. That was worse than someone slicing me open with a blade.

"You were better than Dustin. He was weak—" her mother started, but I turned and glared at her.

"SHUT THE FUCK UP!" I roared. She'd said enough. I never wanted to hear her speak again.

"Don't defend him. He used her," she said.

"I'm *not* defending him! I am protecting her. Shut up! She didn't need to hear it this way. She never needed to fucking know. He's gone. That's over. She had her memories, and she was happy. Don't you see that? What is your problem, woman? Do you enjoy seeing her in pain?"

At least she had the decency to flinch.

"Stop," Sienna said, drawing my attention back to her. "She was right. I should know. That's something I should have been told a long time ago. I don't crumble. I've proved that. It makes sense, really. He was always near her. She was always around. I trusted him. I did. But it makes sense."

There was only emptiness in her voice. I fucking hated it. I preferred her tears. Or even her screaming. But not this. She was shutting down and shutting everyone else out. I wasn't leaving. She wasn't pushing me away.

"I wanted to keep you from being hurt by the Falcos. So I had your aunt check the mail daily and send me all the letters you sent them. I have them all if you want them. I did keep the photos, though. I want them, if that's okay. It was how I watched Micah grow. But the letters, you can take those to Tabby. I have them in the car."

She'd taken the letters because she was punishing us for my brother's cheating. How fucked up was that? My parents lost their son. Then they found out he had gotten Kimmy pregnant, and she'd had an abortion the day after his funeral. It had spread through town like wildfire. A year later Kimmy moved away with a guy and had never returned to Sea Breeze.

Not having to see her had helped. When I saw her face, all I saw was the girl who'd killed my brother's kid. I hated her. I couldn't forgive her. I didn't even want to. She disgusted me.

"Go. Both of you, go. Leave the letters on the porch. I'm not ready for this. Maybe one day I can find a way to forgive you, Mother, but today is not that day."

She didn't look at either of us. Her eyes were still unfocused as she stared off at nothing. "Give me an hour, then please bring Micah home. But I need you to go."

She was talking to me. She wanted me gone.

Fuck no. She wasn't pushing me away.

"I'm not leaving you," I told her.

She sighed, then finally turned to look at me. "Did you know?"

I wanted to lie. I wanted to lie so damn bad.

"Yes." I admitted the truth because I refused to lie to her.

"Then you need to go. I want you to go."

"Sienna, I had my reasons. I was protecting you—"

"I don't care. I want you to go. Leave me. Both of you."

She turned and walked away, locking herself in her bedroom.

I stood there staring at her door, wanting nothing more than to pull it off its damn hinges and make her let me hold her. Explain to her what I had done. Why I did it.

"She needs time. Don't do anything stupid. You never were as stupid as your brother. You were the smart one. Don't let her down, like we did." Then Nina Roy walked away.

I stood in that living room waiting for sobs, or something to give me an excuse to burst into Sienna's room and hold her. There was nothing but silence. She wanted time alone. I would give her that. But this wasn't over. It was the beginning. She just had to see that.

Chapter Twenty-Two

Six years ago . . .

DEWAYNE

"Slow down, man. You gotta calm the hell down. You can't kill her. You'll do life, dude. She's a kid. A dumbass one, but still, she's a kid." Preston's words were falling on deaf ears. I didn't give a fuck. If Kimmy Bart had aborted my brother's baby, I was going to fucking murder her with my own hands.

"Get your ass to the Alpha frat house," Preston said into the phone. "Dewayne's going after Kimmy, and word is she's here. I can't hold him back." I knew I had about five minutes before Rock got here. Because if someone was going to stop me, Rock was the only person I knew who had the strength. I had a slut to find.

I'd lost my brother, and Sienna was just fucking gone. Vanished. And now this shit. I had reached my breaking point, and I didn't give a fuck anymore. Bring on prison. This was all my fault anyway. Fighting with a drunk sixteen-year-old boy had been stupid. He was a kid, and I had threatened him while he was drunk—with the one thing I knew he didn't want to lose. Sienna.

All of this could have been avoided if I'd just walked out of that house and dealt with him when he was sober. Maybe he had been ready to let Sienna go. If he'd been sober and made that decision, then I'd have let him. If he didn't know how lucky he was, then he didn't deserve her. But he didn't have to die over it. That was all me. Fucking me.

"Kimmy's slept with most of the basketball team. Hell, I've slept with her, I think. That could have been anyone's kid. We don't know it was Dustin's. Just because she was claiming it was his don't make it his," Preston said.

I knew this. But I also knew I'd seen my brother fucking her bare. Chances were good that baby had been his. All that was left of my brother, and she'd murdered it. She deserved to die too.

"What if she wasn't even pregnant? Ever thought of that? She was jealous of Sienna. Dustin wouldn't break up with her. He loved Sienna. He just wanted to fuck Kimmy. Girls do that shit when they're desperate. She could have been lying. Don't do life because of a lying teenage girl."

I wanted to blame someone, someone other than me, because the pain and regret were too much. If Kimmy had aborted Dustin's baby, then I could lay all this hate and blame on her. She would deserve it. And I needed to be free of it. I just wanted to take a deep breath again. I wanted to be able to look my parents in the face and not feel like a bastard for being the reason sorrow filled their eyes.

So much pain.

"Where's Kimmy?" I heard Preston ask some guy who stumbled outside.

"Don't know," he slurred.

"Go find her and tell her to hide her sorry ass before Dewayne finds her."

Preston was determined to stop me any way he could. I'd find her, though. I was running out of time before Rock showed up, but I would find her. If not tonight, another night.

"Shouldn't have let you drink so much damn whiskey. Always makes you mean," Preston said, still right beside me. He wasn't helping. All his yakking.

"Hey, Dewayne, sorry about Dustin, dude," a guy called out. I didn't even look at him. His drunken words meant nothing. He didn't know Dustin. None of them knew the real Dustin. They knew the kid with too much pressure to be the best. The kid trying to find himself. They didn't know his heart. None of them did.

"Find Kimmy Bart and tell her to fucking run and hide," Preston called out to him. Dumbass wasn't helping.

"I'll find her. Keep it up. I'll find her and she'll pay," I swore.

"Don't doubt it. I just hope Rock gets here first," Preston replied.

I put both hands on the double doors to the frat house and shoved them open, then stalked inside.

Kimmy came walking down the stairs, looking right at me. Her hair was stringy, and her clothes were wrinkled like she'd just pulled them back on quickly. What the fuck had my brother seen in her?

"You looking for me?" she asked, then stumbled a step and giggled before grabbing the rail. She was fucked up.

"Save yourself and go hide your stupid ass," Preston yelled, purposely drawing attention to the situation.

"Not scared of a Falco. You just tame 'em with pussy," she said, then leered at me. As if I'd even touch that nasty shit.

"Not going anywhere near your nasty snatch," I said, disgust dripping from my voice.

She snarled at me. "What, not as good as sweet little Sienna Roy? You're as bad as him. Can't-do-no-wrong Sienna. Screw that. The bitch sucked at fucking. Dustin hated sex with her. He just did it 'cause she wanted it. But she was awful at it. He came to get the good stuff from me," Kimmy spat angrily.

"I think I just threw up in my mouth," Preston said beside me, and several guys laughed.

"Was that baby Dustin's?" I asked. I didn't want to hear her talk about Sienna again. She wasn't worthy of saying Sienna's name.

She threw up her arms. "He's the only one I fucked without a rubber, and he was the only one I had fucked in months. He and I were going to be an item soon. He just had to get rid of Sienna first."

He was never planning on getting rid of Sienna. He'd killed himself trying to get to her before I could.

"And you killed his baby," I said, needing to hear her admit it.

She shrugged as if what she had done meant nothing. "I wasn't gonna have a baby without a man to help me take care of it. I have my life ahead of me."

That was all I needed to know. I took two steps toward her as the blood roared in my veins. Then arms that could only belong to Rock wrapped around mine and hauled me back against his chest. "Not gonna let you do this," he said in my ear. "You're gonna sleep this shit off, and then you're getting counseling. She's high as a fucking kite. Do you think she would have stopped that while she was pregnant? I can answer that. *No!* She wouldn't have. That baby didn't stand a chance. It would have been born an addict if it had even been born at all."

I glared at her. I hated her. I hated everything she stood for. But he was right. She'd have killed the baby one way or another. She was trash. My brother had made mistakes, and a girl willing to meet his every sexual whim had been his downfall.

"Let's get the fuck outta here," Preston said.

"You gonna walk out of here, or am I gonna have to haul you out? We can fight right here, but I'm sober and I'm gonna win. I won't let you throw your life away over revenge. You have your parents to think about. They need you."

My parents.

I was all they had. Me. The son without the golden halo. The screwup. Me. That was all they had left.

Chapter Twenty-Three

Present day . . .

SIENNA

Had I always known? I sat in the middle of my bed, staring at the wall. Even back then Dustin had been weird when Kimmy was around. And she'd always hated me. I knew she went to the parties he went to. I always thought if they ever did anything, Kimmy would make sure the world knew. But maybe they all knew and no one told me. Because Dustin was their god. They kept his secret.

But why keep it a secret? Why not just break up with me? If he was sleeping with Kimmy and wanted her, then why was he staying with me? Had it always been a friendship between us? Was there ever love between us? Because it certainly wasn't what I felt for Dewayne.

Dewayne.

I wrapped my arms around my stomach as the pain started

again. He had lied to me. I'd trusted him and he'd lied to me. Did everyone lie? Was that the way life was? I couldn't trust anyone but myself.

Dewayne had made me happy. He wanted me, but would I be enough for him? I wasn't enough for his brother. It was possible I wouldn't be enough for anyone. There had to be something wrong with me.

My parents had walked away from me. They'd betrayed me. Dustin had betrayed me in the worst way. And now Dewayne had kept it from me. I expected it of the others, but what hurt the most was Dewayne not telling me.

I wanted to be more important to him than Dustin was. That was selfish and wrong, but it was true. I wanted to be the most important thing to him, because other than Micah, I had been willing to put Dewayne before everyone else. He hadn't felt the same. He had protected his brother's memory. He hadn't wanted me to know the truth about Dustin.

Not to mention all those letters my mother kept away from the Falcos because of this. She didn't want me to be another girl Dustin Falco had left knocked up. In a twisted way I understood her logic. But I had made that decision and, unlike Kimmy, I had been Dustin's girlfriend. Not his secret fuck buddy. It made more sense that I was the one pregnant.

She'd had an abortion. She had aborted Dustin's baby. Images of Micah as a newborn when they'd placed him in my arms flashed before me, and my heart broke. He'd been so beautiful and perfect. He'd looked just like Dustin. Would Kimmy's baby have looked like Dustin too?

Did she ever wonder? Did she care? Or was Dustin Falco and every memory of him a part of her past she rarely thought about? I would remember Dustin every day of my life. My son was my reminder. And I was thankful for it. Even if my memories were tainted. Even if I hadn't been enough for Dustin and he had never really loved me. I had loved him. Maybe not real love, but a pure, young love. And I loved our son. Enough for both of us.

There was a knock on the front door, and I knew Dewayne was here with Micah. I had to pull it together and spend time with Micah until his bedtime. Standing up, I walked to the front door and opened it. Without saying anything, I reached for my son, pulled him into my arms, and hugged him tightly. The feel of his little heart beating was like a balm. He was here. He was my world. I had him. Thanks to Dustin Falco, I had this precious boy.

"I missed you too, Momma," Micah said as he patted my shoulders with his little hands.

I eased my hold on him and pressed a kiss to his head before standing back up. "Go on inside and clean your room. You left it a mess this morning. We'll play Monopoly when you're done," I told him.

He beamed up at me, and I realized it wasn't his father's smile.

It was his smile. His own unique smile. One that was a mixture of Dustin and me. He was part of me. I was a good person too. I had good qualities. Things I hoped Micah got from me.

"Sienna," Dewayne said, and I looked up at him, wishing I didn't have to do this. I wasn't ready to face him yet.

"You lied to me. You protected your brother's memory. I understand that, but I also understand that you chose protecting his memory over me. I need more than that. I need to know I can trust the man I'm with. That he'll never betray me. Maybe that man doesn't exist, and if he doesn't, that's fine. I'm good alone. But I can't do this with you."

Dewayne's face went pale, and the desire to wrap my arms around him and comfort him was strong. But I wouldn't. Today I would protect *me*. I would comfort *me*. It was time.

"I was protecting you. If you'd let me explain. You'll see it was you all along."

No. I wasn't listening to any more. I knew the truth now.

"Leave, Dewayne. You're welcome to visit Micah. He needs you. But for a while it's best you do that at your parents'."

Then I closed the door and locked it.

Micah ran back into the living room with a concerned look on his face. "Where's Uncle Dewayne? Is he not playing Monopoly too?"

No, he wasn't playing Monopoly. That dream was over and he wouldn't be moving in.

"Just me and you, Ace. But we're a good team, right?"

Micah frowned, then nodded. "Yeah, Momma. We are. But I like it when Uncle Dewayne is on our team too."

Three hours of Monopoly up in the center of my bed, a big bowl of mac 'n' cheese, and convincing Micah he needed a shower, and I was exhausted. It was bedtime. I had never needed a rest more than I did tonight.

Micah knew something was wrong. He kept kissing me and hugging me. I needed all those hugs and kisses, but it made me try harder to keep smiling.

"Momma, why is Uncle Dewayne sitting on a sleeping bag on our front porch? Can I go out there with him? I think he has cookies," Micah called from the living room.

What? I dropped the towel I was using to dry my hair and walked into the living room. Micah had his face pressed to the window, waving at Dewayne, who was sitting on a camo-green sleeping bag and eating cookies with a thermos beside him. Had he lost his mind?

"Micah, go to bed. I'll be in there in a minute to tuck you in. I'm going to see if Uncle Dewayne got confused and thinks y'all are camping out tonight," I said.

"Aw, man, that would be fun. I want to sleep on the porch."

I bet he did. "Bed, Micah. Now."

He hung his head and walked back to his room, looking

back longingly at the window. Dewayne could not do this to him. He had to leave. This was messing with Micah's emotions, and I wouldn't have it.

DEWAYNE

She was pissed. Well, she could be pissed. I was going to fucking live on this porch if I had to. The woman was going to listen to me. I wasn't leaving her. I wasn't letting this shit take her away from me. Not when she was finally mine. I wouldn't give her up. This life with her was my future. So she could be pissed. I'd wait it out. I had cookies, coffee, and a sleeping bag. Game on.

"What are you doing?" she demanded as she stepped out onto the porch and closed the door behind her.

"Staying as close to what's mine as I can," I replied.

That affected her. I didn't miss the flash in her eyes before she shut it away. I would take anything she gave me. I just wanted her.

"Micah doesn't understand this. You can't just do this and not care about how it looks to him."

I knew exactly how it looked. One day, when Micah met the woman who would be it for him, who he couldn't live without, I would remind him of this time and he'd know that you fought for what you wanted. You didn't let her go. Women were fucking complicated, but the right one turned the shit in life to gold with a simple smile.

And of course a magic pussy. Probably wouldn't tell Micah about that, though.

"I reckon I'm teaching him a life lesson," I replied, setting my thermos down and standing up. "He'll see that if you love a woman, you fight like hell to hold on to her. And you don't fucking walk away when things get tough."

Sienna went so still I was positive she'd stopped breathing. I wasn't sure what the hell I'd said to put that look on her face, but she wasn't moving.

"Take a fucking breath, Little Red." The woman was trying to scare the shit out of me.

She took a deep breath and shook her head, then turned away to look out at the yard. Then back at me, then back at the yard. "You can't say that," she finally said after all that fidgeting.

"What can't I say, baby?" I asked. Watching her flustered reaction was damn cute. If she wasn't careful, I was going to close this distance she was putting between us.

"You can't, you just can't . . . you can't say that you love me," she said, putting her small fists on her hips and trying to glare at me.

"I reckon I can tell you I love you if I fucking want to. You can kick my ass out of your house. You can be mad at me, and you can make me sleep on this damn porch. But you can't stop me from telling you that I love you. Every single inch of you. I love your smile, your laugh, the way you light up a room, your kindness, your strength, your stubbornness, your fucking magic pussy. I love all of it."

A sob broke free, and then she was crying. Shit!

Screw this space shit. I took three long strides to her and pulled her into my arms. "I tell you I love you and you cry. I ain't that bad. I got some good qualities. Number one being you're the only woman I've ever loved. I loved you when you were a girl, and I love you now. Always just loved you."

She sobbed harder, but this time her hands grabbed my shirt and she held on to me tightly. That was a start.

"I love my brother. But he fucked up. Everything. He made bad decisions and he didn't know what he had. That night, the night he was killed, I went to find him. Heard he was drinking and partying, and he had a game the next day. And I found him with her. I got so fucking angry. He had you. Why would he need anyone else? I said things I shouldn't to a drunk sixteen-year-old boy, and he was coming to you that night because I told him I was telling you. I wasn't letting him do that to you. He panicked and raced out drunk and got behind the wheel before I could stop him." I paused and took a deep breath. The tightness in my chest was there again. That night was a nightmare I would live with my entire life.

"I was about five minutes behind him. I was blocked in at the party, and by the time I got my car out, he'd already wrapped his around a tree. I was too late to save him. I wasn't smart. I got angry and I said things I can't take back."

Sienna wasn't crying anymore. She had gone still and quiet in my arms.

This was the truth. She wanted the truth, and it was ugly. It was something I would never be able to get over. But it was the fucking truth.

"He got behind that wheel. He was the one who got drunk. You didn't make him do either of those things," she said, her head tilted back to look up at me.

I knew that, but I also knew he had been too young to make the right decisions. So ultimately it had been my fault. I hadn't handled it right, and he'd lost his life.

"I loved you then," I told her again. I needed her to understand. For years I had beat myself up about it. I had fucked women. Lots of redheads, trying like hell to forget she ever existed. But my world had lit up like a fucking Christmas tree when she'd walked around that corner in those cutoff shorts. Seeing her again—it had been a jolt I hadn't known I needed. I had just been surviving. Not really living. I was watching my friends live around me, but I wasn't living. I was getting by. Making it day to day.

Sienna made me want to live again. Micah made me want to live. They were mine, and I wasn't letting them go.

"I love you," she said. "I loved you from the moment you found my locker on my first day of high school. I had been so scared and lost. And you'd swooped in and saved the day. I never felt scared when you were around. You made me happy."

The screen door opened, and Sienna jumped into my arms. We both looked over as Micah stepped outside onto the porch, rubbing his sleepy eyes. "Are we camping out on the porch now?" he asked.

Sienna started laughing, then shook her head. "Not tonight, kiddo. Maybe another night. Tonight we're sleeping in our comfy beds."

Micah nodded and looked from Sienna to me, then back to his mother. "Is Uncle Dewayne gonna come inside and sleep too?"

Sienna glanced back up at me. I didn't want her to make this decision just because she didn't want to confuse the kid, but right now I would take whatever leverage I could get. I wanted in my woman's bed.

"Yeah, Uncle Dewayne is coming inside to sleep."

Micah yawned. "You need to get him a bigger bed," he said, then turned and walked back inside. "Come tuck me in. I'm sleepy."

"I'm coming," Sienna replied.

"Uncle Dewayne, too. I want him to tuck me in too," Micah called out from inside.

"We're coming," I said, then winked at Sienna, who just smiled.

Chapter Twenty-Four

Two months later . . .

SIENNA

Because I looked for that girl with the red ponytail to come walking across the street every damn day.

I stopped and picked up the piece of paper on Dewayne's empty pillow. The words didn't make sense. He looked for me to come across the street? When? I stood up and stretched. He'd let me know last night that he had to go to work early this morning. The big condo project that Falco Construction had gotten had a level being completed today. This was important for Dewayne's future. His father had never gotten jobs like this, but Dewayne was taking the business to the next level. I was so proud of him.

I tucked the little piece of paper with the odd note into the pocket of my wrap and went to the bathroom. I'd call him and ask him about it later. Maybe I'd get it once I had coffee. We had gone to bed kind of late last night. He had been unable to keep his hands off me, and I'd enjoyed it very much.

Another little note was on the mirror. I walked over and pulled it off.

Because those big, lost eyes looked at me with trust and lit up whenever they met mine. What was he doing? This was crazy. I read it again and laughed, then tucked it into my pocket before brushing my teeth and then my hair. I didn't have to work today. It was Monday, and I was off. I had to get Micah up and ready, but I'd set my alarm so that I got to drink my coffee before I had to wake up my ball of energy.

I slipped my feet into my furry slippers now that the nights were getting cooler and making the hardwood floors cold in the morning. I opened my door quietly and went to the kitchen. The first thing I noticed was another piece of paper like the others beside the coffeepot.

Because hearing you laugh makes everything okay.

So that one was sweet and made more sense. I got it now. He was leaving me notes about why he loved me. The past two months, Dewayne Falco had become Mr. Romantic. Which was something Preston, Marcus, and Rock thought was the funniest thing they'd ever seen. Dewayne took their ribbing with ease, though. He seemed to like it. I wasn't sure what had happened to him.

Opening the fridge, I reached for the cream only to find another note.

Because you healed me. When no one else could.

I teared up at that one and folded it carefully and added it to the others. That man. I loved him. He didn't see it, but he had healed me too. He had healed my past pain and my bitterness. I'd been able to let it go. Mother was even coming for a visit next month to stay a few days and meet Micah. Life was short, and I was holding something against her and keeping my son from knowing his grandmother. She wouldn't always be there. My father lost his chance to know Micah. But my mother was still here and she wanted to know him.

Reaching into the cabinet, I grabbed my favorite cup, and inside was another note. This was like a surprise scavenger hunt. He knew my morning routine so well. Grinning, I picked it up.

Because you're the most amazing woman and mother I've ever known.

The tears were back. Dang it, I was going to be a crying mess by the time I had to wake up Micah. I sniffed and wiped at my face, then tucked the note with the others. I was going to have to put these somewhere special. Keep them.

I walked over and made my coffee, then turned to the sugar, already prepared to find another note. He didn't let me down. There it was.

Because I can't imagine a life without you.

I wasn't going to cry this time. I fought it back and tucked the note away. He was so getting laid when he got home. The really good wild kind he liked, with me bent over the bed. Maybe even a hell of a good blow job.

I walked over to the table and sat down with my coffee, and just as I pulled out the chair he surprised me again with a note on the seat. I really was predictable in the morning. He even knew which chair to put it on.

Because you and Micah and the other children we will have are my future.

Whoa. Okay. That was . . . wow. I reread it, then tucked it with the others. We hadn't talked about kids. Not ours, at least. We had spent a lot of time with his friends and a lot of time cuddled up talking about life. But we didn't bring up the future a lot. I just knew I wanted him in it. He and Micah were my heart. They filled me up.

Micah's door opened, and he stepped out looking like he'd been awake for a while. Weird. He was grinning like he had the best secret in the world.

"Well, good morning, handsome," I said, opening my arms for him to walk into. He held out his hand instead, and in it was another note. Dewayne had given one to Micah, too.

Because from the time I was seventeen there was only one girl for me.

I sniffed and smiled at Micah. "Did Dewayne give you this before he left or last night?" I asked him, trying to figure out why Micah was up and dressed so early.

"This morning," Micah replied.

Then Micah's door opened again, and Dewayne stepped out of it. He wasn't dressed for work at all. He gave me a sexy smirk and winked. This man was crazy. I loved every bit of his crazy.

"You're here," I said, and Micah moved over to stand beside me just as Dewayne got to me and held out his hand. Another piece of paper.

Because you're mine. And I'm so fucking yours.

I started to laugh and held the note so Micah couldn't see it. I didn't need him saying the F word at school. But Dewayne lowered himself to the floor, and he was on . . . one knee.

Oh my God.

He held out his other hand, and in it was a beautiful princess-cut diamond ring.

"Because I want you to take my last name. Because I want Micah to take my last name. And because I'm nothing without you. Sienna Roy, will you marry me?"

This time I didn't hold back the tears. I let them flow freely as I nodded, then shouted out my "YES!"

Dewayne stood and picked me up and spun me around in a circle while Micah cheered and laughed, watching us. I'd never expected this. I'd never expected him.

No one could have told me that this wonderful, beautiful man would love me like this. I wouldn't have believed them. It was more than I could have asked for.

I couldn't have written a more perfect ending to the story of my life. Because even with all those bad times and moments when I thought things couldn't get worse, the good times and the moments of joy and the love was all so much more. They made it worth it. The journey may not be easy, but when you find the one to take it with, then you can do anything.

ABBI GLINES is a #1 *New York Times, USA Today,* and *Wall Street Journal* bestselling author of the Rosemary Beach, Sea Breeze, Vincent Boys, and Existence series. She never cooks, unless baking during the Christmas holiday counts. She believes in ghosts and has a habit of asking people if their house is haunted before she goes in it. She drinks afternoon tea because she wants to be British but, alas, she was born in Alabama. When asked how many books she has written, she has to stop and count on her fingers. When she's not locked away writing, she is reading, shopping (major shoe and purse addiction), sneaking off to the movies alone, or listening to the drama in her teenagers' lives while making mental notes on the good stuff to use later. Don't judge.

Abbi maintains a Twitter addiction at @AbbiGlines and can also be found at Facebook.com/AbbiGlinesAuthor and AbbiGlines.com.